Advance Praise for
Seven Riddles to Nowhere

"With a fast-paced story and compelling characters, A.J. Cattapan's *Seven Riddles to Nowhere* inspires young readers not only to spend time reading, but also to believe in their own ability to make a difference in this world. Highly recommended for middle schoolers, and the grown-ups who love them!"

—Lisa M. Hendey
author of the Chime Travelers series

"A.J. Cattapan has a knack for getting into the hearts and minds of middle-schoolers. Kids will be hooked from the first page (and parents tempted to read over their shoulders) as they follow an intrepid troop of friends on a quest to save their school. *Seven Riddles to Nowhere* has it all—action, cryptic clues, unique settings, and a hero every kid can root for."

—Stephanie Landsem
author of The Living Waters series

"*Seven Riddles to Nowhere* is a blast, taking the reader on an exciting tour of Chicago streets and churches, while characters gain insight into mysteries and symbols of our faith as they struggle to solve riddles. The tension and suspense mount right up to the very end."

—Theresa Linden
author of *Roland West, Loner*

7 Riddles to Nowhere

A.J. Cattapan

Vinspire Publishing
www.vinspirepublishing.com

This book is dedicated in loving memory of my mother, Marjorie Cattapan, who passed away shortly after it was accepted for publication.

Two of Mom's great loves were children and her faith. She made it her mission to make sure all children knew they were special and loved by God.

May my work as an author carry her mission forward to future generations of children.

CHAPTER ONE

Kameron Boyd hadn't spoken a word in school for seven years. This, however, did not stop his teacher from asking him to stick around after class.

"Mr. Boyd." Mrs. Harris eyed him over the rim of her tortoise-shell glasses. "You'll need to see me after school again today."

Again? Kam's heart sank as he lowered his eyes to his desk. He knew exactly how this after-school meeting would go. The same as all the other ones. Mrs. Harris would talk, and Kam would stand there dumbly, shaking and nodding his head at the appropriate times. When a small movement of the head wasn't enough, he'd scribble a brief note on his whiteboard.

As Mrs. Harris continued discussing the night's homework with the rest of the seventh graders, Kam let his mind wander. There was nothing he could do about staying after school or the impossible homework assignment Mrs. Harris had dreamed up. Besides, he had other concerns on his mind. Like what sort of riddle had his friend Vin—whose full name was Arvin Cheng, but *don't call him Arvin*—texted him just as recess was ending.

The moment the bell rang, thirteen students rushed to grab their jackets and bags from the coat closet. Kam dug out his cell phone, his pulse racing. Vin and Kam were always texting each other riddles and timing each other to see how fast the other could respond with the correct answer. No fair of Vin to send it just as the bell was ringing for class to start up again. He'd been forced to wait all afternoon to see what it was. Riddles should be saved for non-school hours when they could speed-round them.

Before breakfast that morning, Vin had sent a riddle that was easier than a spelling test on three-letter words.

How many animals of each species were on the ark with Moses?

A quick reader would respond "two," but that would be wrong. Kam was a careful reader. He texted back: "None. Noah was on the ark, not Moses."

While munching on his chocolate krispies at breakfast, Kam responded with a riddle of his own while Gram huffed that he spent way too much time on that phone.

Kam shrugged. He *had* to send a riddle back. He owed it to Vin.

What is between heaven and earth?

This one required a bit of thought. Kam wondered how long Vin would take to solve it, but Vin was fast. Before Kam could clear away his breakfast dishes, Vin responded:

The word "and."

Kam grinned. His friend was good. He waited for a new riddle back in response, but when Vin didn't respond right away, Kam figured he would wait until after school. How unfair of him to end up sending it during recess instead!

Now, as his classmates shoveled books into their backpacks, Kam switched on his phone and found the texted riddle from Vin.

Who designed Noah's ark?

"Bet you can't solve that one fast." Vin stood nearby, zipping up his bag.

Kam lifted a shoulder as if already apologizing for his slow response and leaned his head in the direction of the teacher.

Vin glanced at Mrs. Harris before speaking again. "Oh, right. Meet you by the bike rack." He headed out the door with the rest of the seventh grade.

Shuffling around textbooks and spiral notebooks, Kam packed his bag. Among his homework assignments, he stuffed in a letter from the principal that he was supposed to take home today. He tried not to think about the letter too hard. Was it possible St. Jude's might really close? He'd had enough of changing schools and didn't want to think about doing it again.

"Mr. Boyd." The classroom was now empty except for Kam and Mrs. Harris. She sat at her desk, scribbling something in her lesson plan book. When she finished, she looked over the rim of her tortoise-shell glasses. "Come here."

Kam hefted his bag onto his back and then grabbed his notebook-sized whiteboard and dry erase marker.

Mrs. Harris had been a great teacher in the five months he'd been at St. Jude's, but he wasn't looking forward to this conversation. His stomach gave a little lurch.

"I know this oral report assignment frightens you." She adjusted the orange scarf over her purple top.

Kam uncapped his dry erase marker. Frightened wasn't the right word. Not talking in school wasn't a matter of being afraid. It was simply a matter of ability. He scribbled four words on his white board.

I can't do it.

"Kameron." Mrs. Harris tried to look him right in the eyes, but his gaze fell to her wrinkled hands and the colorful rings she wore. "Kameron, you and I both know that's not true. I visited your house, and we had a lovely conversation about your yo-yo competitions. You're perfectly capable of holding a conversation with me."

Kam grabbed a tissue off his teacher's desk and wiped the white board clean.

Mrs. Harris sighed. "I've been doing some research. You're not the only student in the world who has trouble talking in school."

His eyes flickered to Mrs. Harris but quickly returned to studying the cleanliness of his board.

"I'm not a doctor. I can't diagnosis you, but your inability to talk to an adult outside your home sounds a lot like selective mutism. Have you heard of it?"

Kam shook the auburn curls he refused to let his grandmother cut.

"You've heard of being mute, haven't you?"

Mute? Like Helen Keller. Like a mime. Someone who doesn't talk. Kam nodded slowly. He knew what mute was, but that wasn't him. He could talk. At home. Or with friends.

"To be selective is to be choosy. For example, I might select only the best books to read." Mrs. Harris paused. Was he being choosy about the times he couldn't talk? No—why would he choose not to speak in school when some of his previous teachers had wanted to put him in special ed classes with students who struggled far more than he did? No, this was not a choice Kam made. It just...well, it just was.

Kam scribbled on the white board.

Sorry. Really wish I could.

And he meant what he wrote. If he were capable of doing it for Mrs. Harris, who had understood him better than any other teacher, he would do it.

If he could.

But he simply couldn't.

"I had a thought." Mrs. Harris reached inside her right pocket. Although Kam couldn't see what was inside, he knew she was fingering a rosary. Shortly after they'd met, Kam's mom had told Mrs. Harris he was a champion yo-yo competitor and he often kept one in his pocket, something to soothe him whenever he couldn't speak. Mrs. Harris had smiled and said she felt the same way about the rosary in her pocket. And indeed, Kam had seen Mrs. Harris reach for her rosary on several occasions. It seemed to happen most often when she yelled at T.J. Reynolds. No. Not really yelled. Mrs. Harris had more of a deadly calm to her voice when she caught T.J. doing something bad.

Mrs. Harris's fingers twisted around the beads in her pocket. "Perhaps there's another way to prove your public speaking skills. You're pretty tech savvy, aren't you?"

Kam shrugged. He was pretty good with a computer. He wiped his white board and scribbled again.

I'm OK—Vin's better.

"You have my permission to use Vin's help on the technical side, if necessary. Tell me, do you ever make one of those videos, like kids are always posting online?"

Kam scrawled in the corner of the whiteboard.

On YouTube?

"Yes. That's it. The stuff some of them post!" Mrs. Harris clucked her tongue. She looked off into space as if far away in another world. Kam waited patiently until she shook her head and returned her attention to him. "But that is not the point right now. Perhaps we can use this technology for some good. Do you ever make videos?"

He nodded. His mom wouldn't him let post his videos publicly, but he and Vin often made funny game show type videos where they quizzed each other on trivia.

"Wonderful. Since we know you can speak at home, what if you taped yourself giving your speech and then brought it in to show us?"

Now it was Kam's turn to reach inside his pocket and finger the "security blanket" he kept there—his prized 1970 red-and-white Duncan butterfly yo-yo, the one his father used when he'd first taught him.

"You could do that, couldn't you?" Mrs. Harris peered over the rim of her glasses. When she looked at him that way, he had trouble saying no.

But he still had doubts. Sure, he could talk at home. Even doing the speech in front of Vin wouldn't be a problem. But what if, in the middle of recording his speech, he remembered it would be playing in school, in front of all thirteen seventh graders, in front of Mrs. Harris? Would his tongue freeze up? Would his throat tighten and his jaw clench?

Unwilling to give a definite answer, Kam let his head wobble and his shoulders shrug in a way that said, "Sort of. Maybe? I'll try."

Mrs. Harris stood up from her desk. "I'm going to need a firmer answer than that, Kameron Boyd." She bent her nearly six-foot-tall frame until her head came down toward his. She jammed her wrinkled hand deeper into her rosary pocket. Kam fiddled with his yo-yo.

"Kameron." Mrs. Harris touched the tip of his chin with her free hand, and his eyes finally met hers. "You will find, my young scholar, that there are things in this world worth stepping outside our comfort zone for, even if it's only one baby step at a time."

With a silent sigh, Kam reached for the whiteboard.

I'll do my best.

Mrs. Harris's bright red lips curved up in a smile. "That's all I ever ask."

CHAPTER TWO

The wind tossed Kam's curly hair as soon as he opened the heavy rear door of the school.

"Hey, Kameron. Where you going?"

Kam clutched the yo-yo in his pocket. Out of the corner of his eye, he spotted T.J. Reynolds and his friend Marc headed his way. T.J. was a spindly guy, but his buddy Marc was the size of a tenth grade wrestler. Kam scanned the empty parking lot in front of him. The moms in their SUVs and minivans had already picked up the carpool kids, and the walkers had left.

Kam ducked his head and hurried toward the front where Vin would be waiting near the bike rack.

"What? Aren't you going to say hi to us?" Marc yelled. He and T.J. followed Kam toward the school's main entrance.

"Yeah. It'd be rude not to say hi, Kameron. Don't be so disrespectful, dork breath."

Kam sped across the parking lot, but Marc and T.J. matched his pace. The wind picked up, and a strong breeze ruffled Kam's curls. Dark clouds gathered in the sky.

"We're really looking forward to your oral report," T.J. continued. "We're sure it's going to be something we'll never forget."

"Yeah, I can almost hear your speech now," Marc said. "Hold up!"

The footsteps behind Kam suddenly stopped, but he didn't turn around to see what the boys were doing. For a few seconds, the only sound was the occasional crunch of a pebble under Kam's feet.

"Yup, that's what we're gonna hear," Marc said. "Total silence."

T.J. laughed maniacally. "Good one, Marcs-man." The sound of the two boys slapping hands carried across the parking lot. "Hey, wait up, Mute-Meister. We're not done talking with you. We want to hear more of your speech." He laughed, and the two boys must have started running because Kam could hear their footsteps racing toward him.

He looked ahead. Only fifteen more feet till he could round the corner of the building. Then he'd be in sight of Vin, and the two of them could speed off on their bikes. Kam picked up his pace.

Ten more feet.

"We said 'wait up.' Didn't you hear?" A pudgy hand with extra strong fingers clamped down on Kam's shoulder. "Are you deaf as well as dumb?" Marc asked.

As Marc spun him around, Kam pulled the yo-yo out of his pants pocket and into his jacket pocket.

Marc's gaze followed Kam's hand. "What you got in there?"

T.J. poked Kam in the shoulder. "You trying to hide something from us, O Tongue-less One?"

Kam shook his head. His palms went damp, and despite the cool spring breeze, he felt his face heat up.

"Take it out," T.J. yelled.

Kam froze. His hand no longer fingered the yo-yo in his pocket. Marc gripped the edge of Kam's jacket and pulled him closer. "You better take it out, whatever it is. 'Cause we'll find a way to get it out of that pocket, one way or another. Even if we have to flip you over and shake it out."

Visions of being hung upside down on the monkey bars flashed through Kam's head. Back in second grade, at one of his many previous schools, an older boy had tied Kam's shoelaces to the monkey bars and then left him hanging as the recess bell rang.

Slowly, Kam reached into his pocket and pulled out the 1970 red-and-white Duncan butterfly. Maybe if they saw it wasn't money or a phone, they'd let him go.

T.J. snorted. "It's just a dumb old yo-yo." He snatched it from Kam's hand and slipped his forefinger through the string loop.

The idiot didn't even know he was supposed to be using his middle finger. And what did he know about classic yo-yos? Even if it hadn't belonged to his father, Kam still would have viewed it as valuable antique.

T.J. released the yo-yo and yanked at it before it reached the end of the string, causing the yo-yo to swing

erratically under his palm-down hand. Almost impercep-
tibly, Kam shook his head. Some people knew nothing
about the proper way to yo-yo.

"That's not how you do it, moron." Marc seized the
classic toy from his friend. "Ya gotta flick your wrist.
Marc's attempt was only slightly better than T.J.'s. He
still palmed the yo-yo instead of letting it roll off his fin-
gertip, but at least his timing was better with the re-
trieval. The yo-yo almost made it back up to his hand.

"Ah, forget about it." T.J. grabbed it back. "This
thing's so old, it's probably busted." He turned the yo-yo
over in his hand. "It'd probably make a better baseball
than a yo-yo." Lifting his head, T.J. spotted a nearby basketball hoop often used at recess. "In fact, it'd be better
as a basketball."

As T.J. crouched into the stance for a free throw, every
muscle in Kam's body tensed. He wouldn't! He couldn't!

With a nimble jump and a surprisingly elegant flick of
his wrist, T.J. launched the yo-yo toward the hoop where
it bounced off the backboard before dropping in. Kam
ran to the hoop to catch it. He felt like he was in a night-
mare. Time was slowing down, the yo-yo spinning its way
down between the white knots of the basket. His legs pro-
pelling him forward but not fast enough. The yo-yo free-
falling through the air. Kam's hands stretching out to
cushion the falling antique. The yo-yo slipping past his
fingertips and landing on the parking lot blacktop with
a crack, a bounce and then a rattling stop.

"Score!" T.J. raised his hands in victory.

"That was nearly a three-pointer." Marc slapped him
on the back.

Kam stooped to the ground. The yo-yo had split open, and one of the sides had cracked in half. Gingerly, he picked up the pieces. The yo-yo had been the last gift his father had given him. Only days before his father... No, Kam wouldn't think of that day. He wouldn't think of that day ever again. He pushed the memory from his mind.

"What's going on over here?" Sister Maria Ann rounded the corner. She wore her typical black skirt, white blouse, and black blazer. Around her neck, Sister Maria Ann wore a black cord from which dangled a wooden cross the size of Kam's palm. Like most nuns nowadays, she didn't wear one of those black and white veils on her head, a fact that always made Gram a bit nostalgic for "the good old days when everything was simpler."

"Mr. Reynolds. Mr. Greer. What are you still doing here?"

Both boys stopped laughing.

"Nothing, Sister. Just talking to our good friend, Kameron."

Kam turned away from them and concentrated on the broken yo-yo before him. He bit his lip to keep from crying. He wanted to whip around and shove both T.J. and Marc into the muddy pit along the edge of the parking lot. Instead, he pocketed the pieces of his father's old yo-yo, stood up, and turned around.

"Everything okay, Mr. Boyd?"

Could Sister Maria Ann see right through his soul?

Before Kam could nod, T.J. strode up to his side and wrapped an arm around his shoulder. "Oh, yeah, everything's fine, Sister." He gave Kam's shoulder a squeeze. "Isn't it, old buddy?" T.J. shot Kam a warning look.

He needn't have worried. Kam couldn't tell Sister what happened even if he wanted to. Instead, Kam simply nodded at the principal.

"Shouldn't you boys all be on your way home by now?"

Marc answered, "We're waiting for T.J.'s mom to come pick us up. She texted him that she's running late."

Sister Maria Ann jangled the keys in her right hand and looked up at the dark sky overhead. "You better wait inside. Looks like there's a storm coming." She looked to Kam. "Riding your bike home again?"

Kam bobbed his head once.

"You'd better hurry, too. All right, let's go, boys." Sister Maria Ann led T.J. and his sidekick back into the building while Kam raced off to the bike rack.

On the other side of the building, Vin was squirting antibacterial hand gel into his palm—an action Kam must have seen him perform a thousand times in the five months he'd known him. "Where have you been?" Vin rubbed his hands together. "I've been waiting here for precisely twelve minutes and thirty-seven seconds. By my calculations, that's at least six minutes and forty-two seconds longer than your average after-school conversation with Mrs. Harris."

Kam knew his friend used the term "conversation" loosely since only Mrs. Harris ever talked, but it was true that she did often hold Kam after class in order to have a few extra words with him. She must have hoped that when it was just the two of them, Kam might open up and talk.

Kam looked around the driveway and front entrance of the school. No one was around. He coughed to loosen up the vocal cords that had been wound tight all day. "Ran into T.J."

Vin's eyes widened. "What happened?"

Kam pulled out the remnants of the classic Duncan butterfly.

"Your dad's yo-yo," Vin gasped. "Ah, man, that is so harsh. Do you think you can fix it?"

"Probably not. This half's cracked in pieces." Kam spoke more easily now. A raindrop fell on his arm as he re-pocketed the remains of the yo-yo. He looked up at the darkening storm clouds. "We better get going."

The two boys pushed up their kickstands with the edge of their shoes and hopped on their bikes. A quick 180-turn brought them onto the sidewalk that led along the school parking lot. Kam groaned when he looked up. One of the scariest adults he'd ever met was coming down the sidewalk right toward him.

Chapter Three

It wasn't Old Man Engelbert's appearance that made him scary. After all, who could really be frightened of a feeble old man in a motorized wheelchair? It was the way he talked that sent shivers up Kam's spine. His voice had a mechanical sound to it. Almost robotic, but in a deep, husky way. Gram said it came from Old Man Engelbert's forty years of smoking.

Fortunately, Kam didn't have to hear his voice too often. Usually, the old man sat quietly in the back of church every Sunday at eleven and during every single weekly school mass. But when Communion time came, he'd whiz his motorized chair right up to the front before any of the second graders could get out of their pews.

The first time Kam saw it happen, he wondered if the old man was worried about them running out of hosts. Was there a shortage at St. Jude's? But then he saw him do it every Sunday, too. Maybe Old Man Engelbert simply figured his disability entitled him to first dibs. Either way, Kam cringed each time the old man whizzed past and called in his mechanical voice, "Pardon me. Excuse me," as if anyone would dare to step in front of that motorized scooter.

Even the way Old Man Engelbert breathed made Kam vow to stay away from smoking forever. He labored so hard for each breath, Kam swore he could actually hear his lungs working.

In the distance, thunder rumbled. Ahead of Kam, Vin sped up on his bike. Distracted by Old Man Engelbert's sudden appearance on the sidewalk, Kam was a little slower getting started. A sudden gust of wind made pedaling nearly impossible. He ducked his head and pushed down hard on the pedals of the garage-sale bicycle his mom gave him three years ago.

When he looked up again, he noticed Old Man Engelbert's wheelchair had slipped off the edge of the concrete and dipped into the mud pit between the parking lot and the sidewalk. Vin, with his head bent low, dashed right past the old man.

Two more raindrops. Kam looked up. He'd have to hurry if he wanted to avoid getting drenched.

Four, five, six more raindrops.

A few feet ahead, Old Man Engelbert punched at the controls on this wheelchair, but his front wheel simply lodged deeper into the mud pit.

Eight, nine, ten more raindrops.

Kam kept his eyes down to avoid eye contact with the old man as he passed. Pushing into the headwind, he pedaled past Old Man Engelbert, who suddenly threw his wheelchair into reverse. The chair backed up a few inches, right into the edge of the concrete, throwing a spray of mud behind him the moment Kam passed.

Splat! Kam could feel the wet mess oozing down the length of his blue uniform pants. Instinctively, he stopped to inspect the damage. Gram would blame him for the muddy pants. Probably claim he was jumping in mud puddles like he was five years old.

Kam looked behind him. Old Man Engelbert was gonna cost him an undeserved lecture. If Kam were a different kid, he might have had a few choice words for the old man. But Kam wasn't that kind of kid. Instead, he watched Old Man Engelbert spinning his wheels back and forth in the mud. There was no way that old man could get out on his own.

Raindrops began to pelt Kam's head and shoulders. He sighed and hopped off his bike, throwing down the kickstand. He ran the few steps back to Old Man Engelbert. He'd have to do this quickly or the old man might try talking to him.

Grabbing the handles at the back of the chair, Kam yanked the chair out of the mud and back over the edge of the concrete. Before he could let go, a surprisingly strong hand clamped down on his left one.

Old Man Engelbert turned his frail body as best he could to get a look at the one who'd saved him from sitting in mud during a rainstorm. "What's your name, boy?" The old man wheezed. With his left hand, he held a small box over the center of his throat.

Why? Why did I listen so closely to Mrs. Harris's discussion about random acts of kindness?

"I said, what's your name?" The old man's mechanical voice demanded.

Kam shook his head.

"I just want to say thank you." His voice sounded more angry than appreciative.

Kam nodded once, hoping that would be enough to acknowledge the old man's words, and then pulled his hand out quickly. But before he could fully pull away, Kam got a good look at Old Man Engelbert's throat. The old man's wrinkled hand had fallen away from his throat. In the place where he had been holding a small box was now a large, perfectly round, black hole.

CHAPTER FOUR

Kam wanted to run screaming, but for once, his inability to speak in front of adults outside his home came in handy. He hopped on his bike and pedaled like he wore Hermes's winged sandals. The image of that gaping, dark hole in Old Man Engelbert's throat must have jumpstarted his adrenaline because even the steady rainfall couldn't stop Kam from catching up to Vin by the time the boys got to their block.

"What happened to you back there?" Vin blinked away the raindrops falling in his eyes and slicking down his straight dark hair.

Kam pulled alongside him. "Nothing." He wasn't ready to voice his thoughts on the image yet. He needed to process what he'd seen. Maybe it had all been his imagination. People didn't go around with holes in their necks. That wasn't possible. Was it?

Lightning flashed in the sky above. They were almost at the Chengs' large, two-story home where Vin would soon be out of the rain. Kam could see the light on in

Vin's sister's room. Analyn was probably already working on her homework. A few houses down was Kam's
grandmother's house where he and his mom had lived
since last summer when Mom lost her job in Wisconsin.

"You going tonight?" Kam asked his best friend.

"Where?"

"You know, the meeting at school."

Vin raised an eyebrow. "Isn't that meeting for parents? I don't think we're the intended audience." After
five months of being at St. Jude's, Kam was used to his
genius friend sounding like a grown-up. He had, after all,
skipped a whole grade, landing him in the same class as
Kam and Analyn.

Kam shrugged. Vin was probably right, but if St.
Jude's was going to close, Kam wanted to know as soon
as possible. He needed to prepare himself for the torture
of switching schools again. He wasn't sure he could take
it one more time. Five schools in seven years was more
than enough. Maybe he could convince Mom and Gram
to let him go wherever Vin and Analyn ended up. That
way, at least he'd have two friends.

Vin turned into his family's driveway as the rain increased. "See ya later, Kam."

"Bye." Kam ducked his head and pedaled onward. A
few houses down, he reached the house his great grand-
parents had bought shortly after their marriage. Once
upon a time, the house must have seemed quite nice. But
many old homes in the neighborhood had been torn down
and replaced with larger ones so that the Boyd home now
looked crumbly and tiny in comparison.

By the time Kam parked his bike in the back shed, the rain had washed the mud from Old Man Engelbert's wheelchair spinout off his uniform pants. Unfortunately, that also meant he was dripping from head to toe.

"Kameron Alvin Boyd!" Gram shouted as soon as the rear door banged behind him. "What on earth?"

"It's raining, Gram. What do you expect?" His shoes squished as he walked through the mudroom.

"You stop right there, young man." Gram stood in the kitchen, her hands on her hips. Unlike grandmothers in storybooks, Kam's didn't sit around in an apron, baking cookies all day. Gram stood in her workout capris and bright green tank top. "And take off those shoes. You leave all your wet stuff hanging in the mudroom there."

Kam peeled off the dripping jacket and hung it on a hook.

Gram sighed. "It's a good thing I did laundry this morning. Check the laundry basket there for some dry clothes." Gram headed for the kitchen island. From where he stood, Kam could hear her chopping something on the cutting board.

"Is Mom home?" he called as he found a pair of clean sweatpants.

"She's at the library—another one of those workshops on revising your resume. Should be home soon." The chopping noises continued.

When Kam walked into the kitchen, a pile of sliced cucumbers and tricolor peppers lay on the island. Gram was fixing another of her famous vegetable-chocked salads.

"I need to give her this." Kam pulled the letter from St. Jude's out of his backpack.

"More lice?" Gram didn't even lift her head.

"Nah. I think they might close St. Jude's."

"What?" A chunk of carrot flew off the cutting board. Gram had attended St. Jude's herself. So had Kam's dad, which made him a third-generation St. Jude student.

Suddenly, Kam didn't want to talk about it. Gram would go on and on about how many generations of Boyds had been educated at St. Jude's and the tradition would die with Kam. "Here, read for yourself." He threw the letter down on the island and pounded up the stairs to his bedroom.

In his hands, Kam carried the broken pieces of the butterfly yo-yo. He set them down reverently on his dresser next to the framed photo of him and his dad. The picture was taken in the kitchen of their old home in Wisconsin on Kam's sixth birthday, just days before... No, Kam pushed the thought away again. He wouldn't dwell on the past, especially not on that particular day.

An hour into working on his homework, the doorbell rang. Kam, of course, ignored it. Unless it was Vin or someone he knew, he didn't usually answer the door. And Vin always texted before he came over, so it wouldn't be him. Kam went back to working on his pre-algebra problems, but a minute later, Gram knocked on his bedroom door.

"This is for you." She held out a large brown envelope

"What is it?" Kam pulled away from his desk.

Gram shrugged. "Messenger just dropped it off."

Kam took the envelope from her and opened the seal. Nobody ever sent him mail, much less sent something via messenger, but his name was printed on the front of the envelope so it definitely was for him. Who on earth would send him a letter?

Pulling the crisp eight-by-eleven piece of paper from the envelope only added to Kam's confusion. This wasn't an ordinary letter. This was a very official-looking document with a very strange message.

Congratulations!

You are among a select number of heirs chosen to compete in the Seven Riddles Contest!

Solve the riddles.

Find the treasure.

Win the fortune!

At the bottom of the page was information on needing parental consent for contestants under the age of eighteen and the various ways parents could give their consent for their children to participate.

Peering over Kam's shoulder, Gram huffed. "Well, you're not getting your mother's consent for that! It's a scam, for sure."

"But, Gram, it says there's a fortune. Think of it! Mom wouldn't have to worry about finding a job anymore. We could get our own place again." Kam felt a little guilty about that last sentence. Gram had been good enough to take Kam and his mom in when they'd had nothing left, and he did like living with her, but he knew his mom felt like they were just leeching off of her.

"Kam, there's no actual fortune. Scammers send out stuff like this all the time. Just forget about it." Gram turned and went back to preparing dinner.

With a sigh, Kam went back to his math homework. If only life's problems were as easy to solve as pre-algebra.

By the time Kam and his mother arrived at St. Jude's that night, most of the folding chairs in the gym had been filled.

His mother looked around nervously. Since they'd only moved into Gram's house last summer, Mom didn't know many of the people at the parish yet. She knew even fewer people at school since she'd insisted at first that Kam try to "make a go of it" at the local public school. Partly, Kam knew, that was out of pride. Without a job, his mom couldn't afford the tuition.

Of course, out loud, she argued that the public school could do more for him. And that may have been true if Kam had a learning problem. But after three months of Kam's silence in school, the administrators had no better plan than to stick Kam in the classroom with students who needed assistance doing the most basic of tasks. That's when Gram told Kam's mom she'd help pay the tuition at St. Jude's.

Mrs. Boyd tucked her long, dark-blonde hair behind her ear as she scanned the gym for two empty seats. Kam wanted to crawl away. Vin had been right. There weren't any other kids here. And Old Man Engelbert was sitting in the back, his eyes following Kam's movements. Kam looked away but not before sneaking a quick peak at Old Man Engelbert's neck. He couldn't see the hole since the old man wore a scarf wrapped around it. Kam turned from one frightening sight to another: the principal was headed straight toward him.

"Rebecca." Sister Maria Ann placed a hand on his mother's arm. "Is Jackie making it tonight?"

His mom's face turned red. Principals seemed to have this effect on her. Maybe it came from all those years of trying to apologize for her son's lack of speech. "She'll be here as soon as she can. She's got class tonight." "Class" meant the Zumba sessions Gram taught three times a week at the senior center. Kam wasn't sure what Gram was more devoted to—the church, or her workout classes.

Sister Maria Ann fiddled with the wooden cross around her neck. "Well, I hope she gets here soon. Jackie's always been such a strong supporter of St. Jude's, and we need all the support we can get at a time like this."

That didn't sound good. Was the school bankrupt? Would it really close? Kam bit his lip as Sister Maria Ann walked up to the stage. He and his mother slipped into the fifth row from the back.

The meeting began with Sister Maria Ann talking about all the wonderful things that happened at St. Jude's. The students who went on to honors classes at the local high schools. The amazingly high national test scores. The sports programs. The clubs. The foreign language classes and the technology. Standing beside her, the pastor, Father Fitzgerald, nodded in agreement.

Then she stated how the enrollment numbers had declined in recent years. The number of students had shrunk to one-quarter its original size.

Finally, Sister Maria Ann introduced a man who worked for the Archdiocese of Chicago. His name was Mr. DeLuca, and his job was to assess whether or not a school was "fiscally viable." Kam didn't know what that meant, but from the way Mr. DeLuca talked, he was pretty sure it had something to do with money. By the time Mr. DeLuca finished his presentation, many people in the audience were rumbling.

Sister Maria Ann stepped up to the podium as Mr. DeLuca stepped aside. "I know you all have many questions."

A tall man in a business suit stood up. Kam recognized him from Sunday Masses when he and his family always sat in the front row. He was T.J.'s dad, Theodore Jefferson Reynolds III.

"Sister, it sounds like the school is closing. Is that what you're telling us?"

Even from the tenth row back, Kam could see his principal gulp.

"It's possible, Theodore."

More rumblings from the audience.

Sister put up a hand. "But no final decision has been made yet."

"When will it be made?" T.J.'s dad remained standing.

"That's up to the Archdiocese. Perhaps Mr. DeLuca can answer that for you."

Mr. DeLuca stepped forward, scratching the gray hair at his right temple while he considered his response. "The school will have a week to present its plan for the future. If the plan covers for the school's financials adequately, then the school will remain open for the time being. Otherwise..."

"Otherwise," Theodore Reynolds III chimed in, "a week from now, you'll be telling us St. Jude's is closing."

A nod from Mr. DeLuca set the crowd on fire. People turned in their chairs to chat animatedly with the people near them. One woman stood up and crossed the room right toward Fr. Fitzgerald.

Kam slumped in his chair. How could the school come up with a plan to fix their money problems in a week?

For the next fifteen minutes, numbers were recited that meant nothing to Kam—how much the school required to educate the current enrollment, how many new students would need to be added, and how much tuition might be raised if new students weren't added. Or how much money could be saved by consolidating classes. The eighth graders being in the same class as the seventh graders? Kam didn't like the sound of that.

Voices were raised. Fingers were pointed. In the midst of it all, Kam noticed a folded piece of paper sticking out of his pocket—the message about the Seven Riddles Contest. He'd forgotten he'd shoved it in there after dinner. He'd tried during dinner to convince his mom to let him compete, but she'd said it was a scam just like Gram had. But what if it wasn't? What if there really was a fortune to win? Maybe the contest was the answer to saving St. Jude's.

CHAPTER FIVE

"What did I miss, Rebecca?" Gram slid into the seat next to Kam's mom. She still wore her workout clothes from Zumba class, and she breathed heavily as if she'd run all the way from the senior center.

While his mom filled Gram in, Kam decided he'd have to change his mom's mind about the contest later.

The meeting lasted for another painful half hour. Parents were upset. No one liked the idea of combining grades in order to save on costs. Others couldn't afford a tuition hike. Some threatened to leave the school right away and not even wait until the end of the school year. Others begged to start fundraisers, but both Sister and Mr. DeLuca said the school needed much more financial support than some bake sales and car washes could provide.

When the meeting ended, Gram grabbed Kam and his mother and dragged them up to Sister Maria Ann.

"How could the school possibly be in financial danger?" Gram huffed. "There's oodles of money in Winfield Park."

Wondering how best to convince his mom to let him enter the Seven Riddles contest, Kam only half listened to Sister's response—something about Archdiocesan regulations and not being able to depend totally on financial support from the parish. There was also talk about how many of the students came from neighborhoods outside Winfield Park, seeking a better opportunity than their own neighborhood schools provided. Some families could barely afford the tuition, while others were there on scholarship. St. Jude's had become a refuge for students and families who needed an alternative school. Its small class size was ideal for many of these students, but only a few students actually came from the wealthy families of Winfield Park.

While the adults talked, Kam thought about the contest. How many potential contestants were there? How many were kids and would need parental consent? How many would actually get parental consent?

Sister Maria Ann pulled Gram away to talk privately while Analyn and Vin's parents, Mr. and Mrs. Cheng, came up to chat with Kam's mom. As the parents talked, Kam watched as others headed slowly toward the exit, some of them shaking hands with Mr. Reynolds and his wife. Old Man Engelbert used his motorized wheelchair to corner Father Fitzgerald. On the other side of the gym, Mrs. Harris spoke with the science teacher, Mr. Garabini, and the math teacher, Miss Lawton.

For a moment, Mrs. Harris caught Kam's eye. She gave him a brief nod and then slipped a hand into her rosary pocket. Almost subconsciously, Kam slipped his hand into his pocket. The authentic 1970 red-and-white Duncan butterfly yo-yo had been replaced with a new blue one he'd bought before moving from Wisconsin to Illinois. It wasn't the same as having his dad's yo-yo, but he wasn't going to leave home with an empty pocket.

Several families walked out the door together. Among them, Kam recognized Nakia Medina's mom. Nakia was one of those students Sister Maria Ann was talking about when she mentioned students who came from outside Winfield Park. Nakia lived in the city, but her mom brought her out to the suburbs for school because she worried about drugs and gangs in their neighborhood. If St. Jude's closed, where would Nakia go? Would she end up in a dangerous school? Nakia was best friends with Vin's sister Analyn, and he knew she'd be upset if the two of them didn't go to the same school anymore.

"Where will Vin and Analyn go if St. Jude's closes?" Kam's mom asked Mr. and Mrs. Cheng.

Vin's parents exchanged a look. Mr. Cheng rubbed his short, dark hair before responding. "We're not quite sure yet, but we're looking at some schools that are farther away."

Mrs. Cheng nodded. "We really haven't been pleased with some of the other schools around here. It's so hard to find the right environment to challenge Vin."

Kam knew Mr. and Mrs. Cheng wouldn't send Vin to the public school, and that's probably where Kam was headed. Kam would be stuck back at a school without any friends. St. Jude's simply had to stay open. He had to be in that contest, but how could he convince his mom?

As soon as they walked into the kitchen, Kam went into his pitch. "Okay. I know you both think the Seven Riddles Contest is a bad idea. That it's probably a scam, but what if it's not? What if it's for real? And what if it's a lot of money? You know Vin and I are both really good at riddles. We could win this thing, and then donate the money to St. Jude's so it could stay open."

Mrs. Boyd rubbed her temples. "Kam, it's been a long night. Let's drop it, okay? I'm not going to change my mind about this."

"Maybe you should." Gram spoke quietly from a stool at the island. She'd just poured herself a glass of iced tea and was running her fingers up and down its side.

"What?" Kam and his mom said at the same time.

Gram sighed. "I talked with Sister Maria Ann. She knows the gentleman behind the game. Or perhaps I should say *knew* the gentleman behind the game. He's a former St. Jude alum who passed away recently. This 'game' is actually part of his Last Will & Testament. According to Sister Maria Ann, he was extremely wealthy but didn't want his money going to an 'unworthy' heir." Gram drew air quotes around unworthy. "So he's opened up his fortune to only a select number of heirs."

"But how did Kam get selected?" Kam's mom set her diet pop down next to Gram at the kitchen island. "We're not related to anyone wealthy. We don't even know anyone who's died recently."

"Sister Maria Ann wouldn't tell me why Kam was chosen. Simply said the contest was for real, that I could trust her on that, and that neither you nor I should have any qualms about letting Kam participate."

Kam held his breath. Would his mom consent? He could win it. He was sure!

"But why won't Sister tell you how Kam got chosen?"

Gram shook her head. "I don't know, but I've known Maria Ann since our days at St. Jude's together. I'd trust her with my life. If she's keeping information from me, there must be a good reason."

Mrs. Boyd sipped her pop. Kam could tell she was mulling it over. If Kam could just tip her decision in the right direction...

"It's just seven riddles, Mom. What harm could come from that? Just let me try!"

Kam's mom sighed. He rarely asked her for anything.

"Okay. Where do I sign?"

CHAPTER SIX

Kam ran up and hugged his mom. "Thanks, Mom! I'm going to win this. Wait and see!" He leaped up the stairs two at a time.

As he packed up his bag for school tomorrow, he wondered about the seven riddles. What would they be like? Like the ones Vin and he sent each other? Those were easy. Surely riddles worthy of a giant fortune would be harder. Maybe they were logic puzzles. He was pretty good at those, and anything he couldn't solve, Vin could. Maybe the riddles were word games. He'd need Vin's sister Analyn for those. Perhaps they were random trivia questions. No problem. Google and Kam were good friends.

His mind drifted to the treasure. The invitation had said to solve the riddles and find the treasure. Kam's head filled with visions of gold rings and silver chalices. A whole cavern full of them. Yeah, something along the lines of Aladdin's cave.

Kam shook his head as he set his backpack down in his room. He was getting carried away. There was no Aladdin's cave in the suburbs of Chicago. He'd have to wait until the riddles arrived. But how would they come? Via messenger like the contest invitation? Hopefully, they would come tomorrow. Kam wanted to get started right away.

But Kam didn't need to wait for a messenger. By the time he'd packed up his bag and gotten into his pajamas, his phone buzzed. Thinking it was probably Vin wondering why he hadn't solved the last riddle yet, Kam readied himself to reply, but it wasn't a text from Vin. The text came from a number he didn't recognize, and his heart pounded as he read the message.

> Welcome to the Seven Riddles Contest! You've been cleared for participation. Are you ready for your first riddle?

Kam blinked at the screen. How'd they get his phone number? He texted back:

> Yes, but who are you?

A moment later, he got a response.

> You can call me the Master Riddler. Here's riddle #1: For whom should we ask St. Procopius to pray?

What? Kam stared at his phone like the message had been written in Mandarin. What kind of a riddle was this? No logic question. No word play. Perhaps Gram could help. She was good with church stuff.

Kam jumped off his bed and headed down to the kitchen where his mom and Gram were still talking.

"Hey, Mom, did you give your consent already?"

"Yes, the direction said I could email it over. Why?"

"I got a riddle on my phone already."

Both Gram and Mom jumped up from their stools. "You did?" his mom asked.

"Yeah, but how'd they get my number?"

Gram shifted a little. "I gave it to Sister Maria this evening. She said she'd pass it along if Mom gave her consent."

"Well, that was fast!" Kam's mom said. "What's the first riddle?"

Kam showed them his phone, but his mom just pulled her eyebrows down low over her eyes as she squinted at the text. Gram wasn't any help either. "Sorry, Kam, I have no idea who St. Procopius was."

"Maybe I can Google him," Kam said.

"Uh, not tonight, young man." His mother folded her arms across her chest. "You've been up long enough tonight. Go get some sleep."

Kam's shoulders slumped. He didn't try fighting his mom on this one. The computer was in the den, and she'd never let him use it this late at night. He'd just have to Google St. Porcupine, or whatever his name was, in the morning.

In the bathroom, Kam brushed his teeth. He was so deep in thought over the riddle and the Mystery Riddler that he was surprised to find his gums bleeding. Looking at his reflection in the mirror, he stared at the thin red lines oozing near the top of his teeth. What a crazy day. First, Mrs. Harris assigned an oral report. Then T.J. broke his dad's yo-yo. Now St. Jude's could be closing, and some guy—girl?—was sending him strange riddles. Maybe things would make more sense tomorrow.

As soon as the alarm went off, Kam bolted out of bed. He'd set it extra early so he'd have time to Google St. Porcupine—or was it St. Precipice?—and finish his math homework.

With his backpack slung over his shoulder, Kam crept along the upstairs hallway. Mom was still in bed, the rounded shape of her blankets hunched in the dim morning light. Gram had the big bedroom in the corner not far from the stairs. Her bed was already made. No doubt Gram was out for her pre-breakfast walk.

Without turning on a light, Kam punched the computer's power button. Hopefully, the computer's tweeps and beeps wouldn't wake Mom.

Once he was online, Kam reread the riddle on his phone.

Riddle #1: For whom should we ask St. Procopius to pray?

Double-checking the spelling, Kam punched the name into the search engine. The first link was for a St. Procopius Abbey somewhere downstate Illinois. Useless. The next few links were encyclopedia articles. Kam grinned. He'd have his answer in no time. All he needed was to find out what St. Procopius was the patron saint of. Maybe he was like Saint Anthony, and people asked him for help finding lost items.

Kam clicked on the first encyclopedia article, and his smile vanished. There had been three saints named Procopius. Who would've guessed that name had been popular once upon a time? Each listing was another link that led to a very short biography. The first was Saint Procopius of Scytholopolis, the name of which reminded Kam a bit of Superman's home of Metropolis. He was a martyr and might have been either a soldier or a prince, depending on which legend you believed, but there was nothing about him being a patron saint or what kind of person we should ask him to pray for.

The second link sent Kam to a super-short biography for Saint Procopius of Sazava, a Czech saint who lived as a hermit during the eleventh century.

The third link was for Saint Procopius of Ustug, a Russian Orthodox saint who died in 1303. He had been born a Roman Catholic in Germany but later converted to the Eastern Orthodox Church. Kam didn't know what all that meant, but he was certain of one thing—he had no idea who he was supposed to ask Saint Procopius to pray for. Maybe he was crazy for trying to solve these riddles. If he couldn't get this first one, how would he ever get the rest?

A key scraped its way into a lock. Kam looked up to find Gram walking in.

"What are you doing up this early?"

Kam pointed to his phone. "Trying to solve the riddle."

"Any luck?"

Kam shook his head. Maybe he was a fool to think he could win this fortune. He'd have to text the Master Riddler back and admit defeat. He was crazy to ever think he could save St. Jude's.

CHAPTER SEVEN

Saving St. Jude's was all anyone talked about at school. Every class period began with students drilling the teacher about last night's meeting and what they thought would happen to the school.

The teachers all said the same thing. "Nothing's decided yet. We have to wait and see what plan the school can come up with and if the Archdiocese will accept it."

The teachers changed topics quickly as if it were no big deal, but Mrs. Harris reached into her rosary pocket several times and Miss Lawton had to grab a tissue for her "runny nose" before reviewing the pre-algebra homework.

At lunch, Kam took his usual seat next to Vin in the noisy but not very crowded school basement. Across the table from them, Analyn blabbed on and on about how St. Jude's couldn't *possibly* close. "It'd be a travesty, a tragedy, a complete disaster. This place is an institution in Winfield Park. What is the Archdiocese thinking?"

Analyn's best friend Nakia pushed her long dark hair behind her shoulders. "They're just doing their job. After all, schools need money."

"So all they care about is their profit?" Analyn's hands flew up in disgust.

Nakia shook her head calmly. "No, but they have bills to pay."

Analyn dropped her hands. "If only there were some way to give St. Jude's the money it needs."

"Yeah, like win the lottery," Nakia said.

Vin looked up from his bologna sandwich. "The odds of winning the Illinois State Lottery are one in 176 million."

"What my brother's saying is we'd have better luck if we planted a few dollar bills and waited for them to grow into money trees."

Vin scrunched up his nose. "That's not exactly what I'm saying."

"Oh, stop taking me so literally all the time." Analyn stirred her yogurt. "Of course, we could buy a whole bunch of lottery tickets and that would increase our chances."

Vin shook his head. "You aren't old enough to play the lottery."

Analyn gave her brother a sour look as Kam took another grape from the bunch Gram had put in his lunch. Should he tell them about the contest? The Master Riddler hadn't said anything about not asking for help. In fact, how would the Master Riddler even know if Kam talked to his friends about it?

Of course, talking at the moment wasn't even possible. Kam looked up as today's lunch monitor, Mr. Garabini, sauntered past their table. No, if he were going to ask for help from his friends, it would have to wait until they were alone at recess.

When they were let outside, Kam gestured for Vin, Analyn, and Nakia to follow him past the playground equipment. There was a spot on the field not far from the creek that marked the school's western border where the recess monitors never walked. It was here Vin had first discovered Kam *could* indeed talk—as long as no adults came their way.

"What's up, Kam?" Analyn's eyes were wide. Kam rarely motioned for her and Nakia to follow him and Vin to their quiet spot.

Kam took a deep breath. "I may have a way to save St. Jude's."

Analyn and Nakia blinked in surprise, but Vin seemed the most incredulous. "How? I know you didn't win the lottery."

"No." Kam's hands grew sweaty as he pulled a folded piece of paper out of his pocket. "A messenger stopped by my house last night and brought me this." Kam showed them the invitation to join the contest.

Analyn reached for it and began to read it aloud.

"Shh!" Kam shushed her. "Don't let anyone else hear."

Analyn lowered her voice and finished reading it while Kam kept his eye on the rest of the playground. No one was near enough to overhear them.

"Is this real?" Nakia asked. She had a quiet, calm way of speaking, quite different from Analyn's loud and dramatic voice befitting a future career in the theater.

Kam nodded. "Gram talked about it with Sister Maria Ann last night after the meeting. I didn't think my mom was going to go for it, but she did, and then I got this riddle right away last night."

Kam pulled out his phone and showed them the first riddle.

"Who is this guy?" Analyn asked.

"I looked up the phone number this morning. It's a cell registered to someone here in Winfield Park."

Vin rolled his eyes. "Well, that only limits the field to..."

"I know," Kam said. "Way too many for us to check into all of them." His hands shook. What if they thought this whole idea was crazy? Too late now. He'd already started.

By the time he finished describing his search results on St. Procopius, Vin had whipped out his own phone and was shaking his head. "I'm getting the same results Kam did." He shoved his phone back in the pocket of his blue uniform pants. "What a ridiculous riddle. If Wikipedia doesn't have the answer..."

"Maybe you need to go to St. Procopius," Nakia said it as if she were suggesting visiting the local movie theater.

Analyn scrunched up her nose. "You mean find where the saint with the crazy name is buried?"

"Not St. Procopius, the person. St. Procopius, the place."

An image of Kam's early morning search results flashed before him. "St. Procopius Abbey? That's way downstate."

Nakia shook her head. "No. St. Procopius Church. It's in the Pilsen neighborhood near my Aunt Talia's house. I was there a few weeks ago for my little cousin's Baptism."

Kam didn't know where the Pilsen neighborhood was. He knew his old Milwaukee neighborhood far better than Chicago.

Nakia, on the other hand, lived in the city and knew a lot more about it than he did.

"Is the church near your house?" Analyn asked the question on Kam's mind. He didn't think the Chengs' knowledge of Chicago neighborhoods was much better than his. From what he could tell, they'd lived a pretty sheltered life in Winfield Park.

Nakia bit her lip. "Maybe twenty minutes from my house."

Vin had his phone out again. "Whoa, it's way down *there*?"

Four heads huddled over the phone. Vin had pulled up a map of Chicago with the address for St. Procopius Church pinpointed.

A spiky-haired shadow fell over the four friends. "What stupid YouTube cat video are you watching now?" T.J. sneered down at them.

Vin slipped the phone back in his pocket. "I don't see how that's any of your business."

"Everything that goes on at St. Jude's is my business. My dad practically runs this place."

Kam nearly snorted. Theodore Reynolds III was the parish's financial advisor, but he wasn't the principal.

"What do you want, T.J.?" Analyn sounded bored.

"I got a question for Nakia."

The Chengs and Kam turned to the quiet girl as if she'd suddenly become a traitor to their little foursome.

Nakia, ever calm, gave a little nod. "What's your question?"

"You know all sorts of religious stuff, right? I mean, your mom burns all those Jesus and Mary candles."

Kam wished T.J. would go away, but if he was looking for answers to religious questions, he had come to the right person. Nakia always scored the highest on their religion tests.

"What do you want to know?"

"Have any idea what St. Procopius is known for?"

Luckily, T.J. was looking only at poker-faced Nakia when he asked the question. Otherwise, he would have seen the other three exchanging glances.

"Which one?"

"What d'ya mean, which one?" T.J.'s face flushed with anger.

"There were three of them."

"Three?" T.J. stomped his foot. "Fine. Tell me what all three of them were known for."

Kam held his breath. Would Nakia tell him about the church? It couldn't be a coincidence that T.J. was curious about the same saint.

"There's not much to tell. At least one was a martyr, and they all lived a really long time ago."

"But what did they do? Did they help a certain group of people?"

"One of them moved to Russia." Nakia lifted her voice at the end as if to say, *Does that help?*

T.J. nodded. "Russia. Yeah, maybe that'll work." Without another word, he ran back to the kickball game in progress.

When he was out of earshot, Analyn leaned forward. "Kameron, is T.J. in this contest, too?"

"Could be."

Vin nodded. "Why else would he be asking about St. Procopius? He's not exactly common."

"But how could we both be in the same competition to inherit a fortune? We're not related."

"What do you mean?" Analyn asked.

Kam shared how Gram had explained that the game was really part of a Last Will & Testament, and that some unknown relative of his must have died, but neither his mom or grandma had any idea who.

"So this is like the *The Westing Game!*" Analyn exclaimed.

"The what?" Kam asked.

"*The Westing Game*," Analyn repeated. "A book we read in fifth grade. This guy died and had to leave his fortune to someone, but he wanted it to go to the worthiest person, so he set up a will that involved a bunch of clues. Whoever solved them got the inheritance."

Kam looked at Analyn, horrified. "But that would mean I'm related to T.J.!"

Analyn had her hair pulled into its usual one-sided ponytail. It was an asymmetrical look that drove Kam crazy. In his opinion, the world needed more balance.

Analyn twirled the ponytail around her finger before answering his question. "Perhaps, but maybe it's one of those really, really distant relative kind of things. Or a half-sibling. Or maybe there was adoption involved in there somewhere."

Vin looked at Kam and then rolled his eyes at his sister's suggestions.

The bell rang, signaling the end of recess. "I don't know exactly how you're related." Analyn stood up and smoothed her plaid skirt, dusting off the dried leaves that clung to it. "But I know this much. You can't let T.J. get to that treasure first."

CHAPTER EIGHT

The plan had to be formed quickly. The answer to the riddle had to be at St. Procopius Church. Getting there, however, would take time. That meant waiting until Saturday and having Nakia join them. She knew the church's location and was far better at getting around the city.

Nakia would ask her mom if she could sleep over at Analyn's house on Friday night. Then they'd leave early Saturday morning.

Vin suggested asking an adult for help.

Kam shook his head. "My mom barely agreed to let me join this contest. I don't think she's going to take us into the city. Besides, she's got another job fair this Saturday, and Gram has a Zumba class to teach."

Analyn said. "And it's not exactly like we can wait. We can't let T.J. solve these riddles first. He'd never donate the money to the school. He'd spend it all on dumb video games."

As much as Kam hated the thought of the four of them going into the city alone, he agreed with Analyn. It was the only way to beat T.J. and possibly save their school from closing.

⌒

On Friday, Kam kept his eye on T.J. who seemed frustrated most of the day—always scratching his head and not making nearly as many snide remarks as usual. Kam took this as a good sign. If he'd solved the first riddle, he would've looked much happier.

At recess, the four friends continued making plans.

"Can we even get into a church on a Saturday?" Analyn asked.

"Most churches have Saturday morning Masses," Nakia said.

Vin took out his phone. "Let's see if the parish has a website." In seconds, Vin smiled, but his grin quickly faded. "Hey, most of their website's in Spanish."

Kam suppressed a chuckle. Spanish was the one class his genius friend didn't ace.

"Of course it's in Spanish." Nakia leaned over Vin's shoulder. "I told you it was in the Pilsen neighborhood."

Vin leaned away from Nakia as if her "girl cooties" might be contagious. "Yeah, so?"

Nakia stopped reading over Vin's shoulder. "Pilsen has a huge Mexican immigrant community. Here." She held out her hand. "I'll translate."

Vin reluctantly turned over his phone. With a Mexican mother and a Spanish/Egyptian father, Nakia breezed through Spanish class.

"On Saturday mornings, there's a Mass in the little chapel."

"Is that where we need to go?" Kam asked.

"Who knows? But the parish office is open at 9:00. Maybe we can find someone to let us into the church."

Kam knew there was no way he could convince an adult to let him into a church. He wouldn't be able to say a word. But if anyone could talk their way into a place, it was Analyn.

"So how do we get there?" This was Kam's biggest worry.

Nakia had an answer for that, too. "Well, if we're leaving from the Chengs' house, we'll have to take the purple line, transfer to the red, and then get on the blue line once we're downtown."

Nakia's instructions sounded like coloring directions.

"The purple line of what?" Kam asked.

"The 'L,' silly."

"Oh," Analyn and Vin said at the same time.

Kam shook his head. "I'm still not getting it." As far as he knew, "L" was simply the twelfth letter of the alphabet.

"It's the subway system in Chicago," Analyn explained.

"Then why do they call it the 'L'?"

"Because a good part of it isn't underground at all. It's actually elevated above street level. The 'L' comes from *el*-evated."

The recess bell rang, and the four friends stood up.

Nakia tucked her white uniform shirt back into her plaid skirt. "I guess this means you guys don't have your own CTA passes, huh?"

Blank looks greeted her. In return, she gave one of her rare smiles. "Okay, then, my suburban friends, bring some dollar bills tomorrow."

Chapter Nine

When Kam got home from school, his phone buzzed—another text from his secret messenger.

Solved the first riddle yet?

Up in his room, Kam typed a quick reply.

No. Going to St Proc Church tomorrow to search for answer.

After setting down the phone, Kam tried brainstorming famous people for his oral biography report. He didn't know what famous person he should talk about. He also still didn't know if Mrs. Harris's video plan would work. Maybe she'd accept a typewritten report if he choked up in front of the video camera.

The phone buzzed again.

Better hurry or another will find the treasure.

Not needing more pressure, Kam decided not to reply. He was already feeling lousy about the whole thing. Nakia was the one who came up with the idea to visit the church. Analyn would be the one to talk their way into the building. Kam could never speak to strangers like that. What good was he? He was doing nothing to solve this riddle.

And then there was that report due in Mrs. Harris's class. He didn't even have a topic yet. He was supposed to speak on someone famous, but no one good was coming to mind.

Kam set his alarm for early the next morning. They planned to leave Winfield Park around seven.

When the alarm went off, Kam groaned and shut it off quickly. He didn't want it waking his mom or Gram. After a breakfast of cold cereal and juice, he slipped on his jeans and a t-shirt. He threw on an old hoodie, too. The thermometer outside the kitchen read fifty-five degrees. It was a cool spring morning.

In the den, he pulled out a piece of paper and a pen to write his mother and Gram a note, but he was only halfway finished when Gram came through the back door in jogging pants and a windbreaker. Kam cursed himself for not having set the alarm a little bit earlier.

"What are you doing up so early?" She spied the backpack on his back. "And where are you going?"

Kam gulped. "I was leaving you and Mom a note. I'm headed over to Vin's house. We're working to see if we can't come up with any answer for that riddle and maybe work on some more school stuff." He indicated his backpack.

"This early in the morning?"

"We've got a really big project."

"And what exactly is this project?"

Why did Gram always have to be so nosy?

"It's a biography report. We need to record ourselves, so Vin said he'd help me out." Like the note he'd planned on leaving, Kam was sort of telling the truth. They did have a biography report, and going to St. Procopius was sort of a school project—if you counted saving the school from closing as a project.

Gram picked up Kam's cereal bowl from the table. "I see you've had breakfast." She humphed. "Couldn't have bothered putting away your dirty dishes though, could ya?"

"I was going to do that as soon as I finished the note." That part was totally true.

Gram set the dirty bowl in the dishwasher. "How long is this project of yours going to take?"

"Probably pretty long. I'll miss lunch." Kam rolled back and forth on the balls of his feet. Was Gram going to let him go? What if she didn't? What if she insisted he come home for lunch? Could they even make it to St. Procopius and back by then?

"Be home in time for dinner." Gram had her back to Kam. He couldn't see the look on her face, but her voice didn't have its usual snap.

"Thanks, Gram. See ya later." He reached for the back door and then stopped. "Gram, if St. Jude's closes, can I go to whatever school Vin and Analyn go to?" Maybe if St. Jude's closed, he could at least be at the same school as his friends.

Dishes clinked in the kitchen before Gram responded. "I don't know about that, Kam."

"Why not?" He adjusted his backpack. "I'm sure Mrs. Cheng would give me a ride if it's too far away."

"It's not that, Kam." Gram kept her eyes on the coffeemaker.

"Then what?"

Gram sighed before turning to him. "I don't think we can afford the tuition anywhere else."

"But you pay for the tuition at St. Jude's. The other Catholic schools can't be that much more."

Gram shook her head. "We don't pay tuition at St. Jude's."

"Huh?"

"When the public school told us what they had planned for you, I asked Father Fitzgerald and Sister Maria Ann if they could help out. Money's been tight. Teaching Zumba barely pays the real estate taxes in this neighborhood."

"So, what—I'm like on scholarship or something?"

"Not exactly. When I approached the school for help, the housekeeper at the rectory had just resigned. I've been doing the cooking and cleaning for Father Fitzgerald in exchange for tuition."

Kam gulped. He pictured Gram cleaning toilets for the pastor.

"Gram—" He didn't know what to say.

Opening a kitchen cabinet and pulling down a mug, Gram said, "Don't worry about St. Jude's, Kameron. God will provide." She looked him in the eye. "Go work on your school project."

Wanting to say more but not finding the right words, Kam headed out the back door and trudged over the lawn to the shed.

A few minutes later, he was pedaling his bike to the Cheng house. His three friends stood out front. Analyn and Vin had new hybrid bikes. Kam's bike was rusty and outdated by comparison, but at least it wasn't the pink princess bike Nakia sported.

Analyn threw up a warning hand as soon as Kam caught sight of it. "Don't make fun of her. It's the only spare bike we had."

"What did you tell your parents?" Kam asked.

"I told them the four of us are working on a school project together."

Vin shoved his phone in his pocket. "Let's get going. According to my calculations, we've got 1.83 miles to the 'L' station."

In the crisp spring morning air, the four amigos pedaled down several side streets before turning onto the sidewalk along a main road. Kam was glad he'd worn his old hoodie. The April breeze sent shivers down his spine.

After locking up their bikes, they entered the train station which looked like a run-down news stand hidden underneath the elevated tracks. Inside were several vending machines that spit out transit cards instead of candy. Nakia showed them how to insert their dollar bills in exchange for the paper tickets with a black stripe on one side.

She was in the middle of helping Analyn get hers when the building above them began to shake. Kam considered running for cover as the loud rumbling increased and a loud shriek pierced the air.

Nakia looked up. "We won't make this one," she shouted above the noise. The rumbling softened as the screechy brakes brought the train to a stop above their heads. By the time all of them had their cards, the first train had rumbled out of the station.

At the turnstiles, Nakia showed them the correct way to insert and remove the transit cards. Luckily, the station was empty when Kam tried walking through the turnstile before removing his card and ran stomach-first into the locked turnstile. He blushed as he pulled out the card and pushed his way through. How many more mistakes would he make today?

A long flight of metal stairs led up to the train platform. Kam's stomach churned. Was riding a train above ground safe? They didn't have elevated trains like this in Milwaukee. They didn't even have a subway.

In her usual quiet but confident way, Nakia led the charge up the stairs with Analyn close at her heels.

Kam grabbed Vin's sleeve before they followed the girls. He had something to say and worried the presence of adults on the platform would slam his throat shut.

"Hey, you haven't figured out how dangerous these things are or how many people get mugged on them every year, have you?"

Vin shook his head. "No. Although, maybe it's better that I didn't." He reached into his pocket for a small bottle and squeezed some gel into his hands. "The germ

count in this place alone is enough to scare me to death."
He pocketed the antibacterial lotion and then rubbed his
hands together.

Kam didn't want to think about the germs. Finding
ways to talk with his friends when there were so many
adults around would be problem enough.

Chapter Ten

Emerging onto the train platform, Kam surveyed his surroundings. They were at least a full story above the ground, and the wind whipped across the empty train tracks. A few adults and one toddler waited on one side of the platform. On the other side, Nakia and Analyn found seats on a bench. Above their heads was a sign with the station's name and purple stripes, appropriate for a route called the purple line.

On the other side of the tracks were the rooftops of the pizza place and the dry cleaners they'd passed on their bicycles only a few minutes earlier. The raised platform put them up among the trees, and with nothing but a sheer drop on the other side of the tracks, Kam felt exposed.

"How long will we have to wait?" Analyn asked, as Kam and Vin joined the girls on the bench.

Nakia lifted one shoulder. "Shouldn't be too long. The trains come pretty often." She swung her short legs under the bench. Kam admired her total calm.

"So what exactly are we going to do when we get there?" Vin asked.

"Find someone to talk to, of course." His sister tightened her usual one-sided ponytail. "Someone who's an expert on St. Procopius."

"Maybe there's a clue inside the church," Vin said. "You know, something that tells us what he was known for."

"That is so typical of you, Arvin. Why do you always have to do things the hard way? Why not ask someone for help instead of doing it all by yourself?"

"Not everyone is as chatty as you are. I'm sure the priests at St. Procopius have better things to do than give you the biography of their patron saint."

"If they work there, they should know something about the saint, and why wouldn't they want to tell us?"

Kam wanted to sink into his seat. If the Chengs got into one of their historic fights again, this was going to be a really long trip.

A distant rumbling made Kam turn his head. The flat-fronted car of an 'L' train rattled its way toward them. Kam started to stand, but Nakia grabbed his arm. She shook her head at him. "That one's northbound," she shouted over the increasing din. "We want one going the other way."

Kam sank back onto the bench. At least the noise of the train had stopped Vin and his sister from fighting. The family on the other side of the platform stepped onto the train. Several people got off. One college-aged boy wore a Northwestern University sweatshirt. A couple older women in workout gear chatted as they headed down the stairs, followed by a man in a business suit.

As the commuters walked down to the street level, a few families climbed up. One of the fathers grumbled something about not being able to watch the Cubs' game. Behind the families were two teenage boys in black jeans, black t-shirts, and body piercings in places that had to be painful.

Another loud rumbling caused all four St. Jude's students to sit upright. Nakia leaned over to look past the families now standing on the platform.

"This is us," she declared and stood up. Following her lead, Kam waited a few feet from the platform's edge while the train came to a screeching halt. When the doors slid open, a few riders trickled out and everyone waiting hopped on. The teenage boys got on the car in front of them, but the families got on the same car they did.

Kam took a seat on one of the hard plastic chairs not far from the door. Vin sat down next to him but only after inspecting the chair for gum. The girls sat across the aisle.

Through the window above Analyn's head, Kam saw two elderly gentlemen heading toward the train. They walked briskly, especially for two old men. They both wore beige trench coats, and one carried a cane. They looked like they were about to get on the same car as Kam, but at the last minute, the taller of the two grabbed the shorter one's arm and yanked him into the car ahead of them.

Something like a doorbell sounded, and a recorded male voice said, "Doors closing." The robot voice didn't lie. The sliding doors closed immediately, and the train gave a little lurch.

As the train's speed increased, Kam gazed out the large square window, watching the trees fly past faster and faster. Across the aisle, the two girls chatted, but the whirring of the train made it impossible to eavesdrop. That was fine with Kam. Watching the city from above street level was fascinating. Why hadn't every city built trains up high? It saved road space, and you got a view no one ever saw from a car.

At each stop, the doors slid open, the doorbell chimes sounded, and the mechanical voice announced the location.

When the robot voice announced, "Next stop is...Howard," a few people on the train stood.

Nakia leaned across the aisle. "This is where we change to the red line."

Apparently, the Howard stop was the end of the purple line, as everyone filed out of the cars. A few headed to street level, but the rest made their way onto a red train, including the families, the black-clad and body-pierced teenage boys, and the two old men in trench coats.

The trip on the red line was much longer. Kam soon let his body sway to the train's rocking motion. He loved the way the tracks sometimes seemed to hang suspended over nothing as if he were gliding along through the trees like a bird. The train turned to follow its weaving path through the city buildings.

After a half-hour, the tracks slanted down before hurtling through a dark tunnel. So much for being elevated all the time. This part of the ride was not as appealing. The dark tunnels with their fluorescent lights speeding past made Kam feel like he'd been buried alive.

At an underground station named Jackson, Nakia led them off the train.

"Where are we going now?" Analyn asked.

"See these signs?" Nakia pointed to one that hung over a set of stairs. "Blue Line. We're getting on one of those."

The stairs led deeper underground, and Kam wondered how many feet of dirt and concrete lay above his head. At the base of the stairs, they turned right into a tunnel lined with millions of small white squares. Overhead, the tunnel arched, and the monotone of the white was broken by a few blue and red stripes.

After a minute of walking, Kam wondered if the tunnel would ever end. He looked at Analyn and Nakia who walked in front. Over their heads, an LCD sign thanked them for riding the red line and reminded them that there was no smoking on CTA property.

Looking back to see how far they'd come, Kam thought he saw the two old men who'd hurried onto the train back in Winfield Park. He couldn't be quite sure because there were too many people in the tunnel. Kam shook his head. No, they probably weren't the same men. Lots of old guys wore beige trench coats and those flat caps that made them look like boys who sold newspapers a hundred years ago.

An upward flight of stairs brought them to a new underground platform, this one dominated by blue signs.

They didn't have much time to look around. A car arrived and Nakia pushed them on before the doors slid shut.

Kam looked at his watch. The trip had already taken an hour. If they didn't get there soon, Mass would be over and the church might be locked. As the train began to pick up speed, Kam caught a glimpse of the flat caps again. One of the old men shook a fist at the train as it pulled away. The other one caught Kam's eye, and his mouth moved, making his mustache twitch. Was it his imagination, or were they being followed?

CHAPTER ELEVEN

Four stops later, Kam and company stepped off the blue line. They were above ground and, from the looks of it, smack dab in the middle of an expressway. To the right and left of them were train tracks, and beyond the tracks, cars defied the speed limit.

"How on earth do we get out of here?" Vin screeched.

"This way." Nakia led the boys and Analyn up a ramp to a bridge and then turned right. "My parents and I took the blue line from our neighborhood over here for my cousin's Baptism. It's about a ten-minute walk now."

"What?" Vin cried.

Kam checked his watch. No way they'd make it to the church before morning Mass ended. It'd been an hour and a half since they'd left home.

Nakia's idea of a ten-minute walk turned into nearly twenty minutes. She shrugged when Vin questioned her time estimation skills. "It seemed like only ten minutes when I walked it with my family."

They rounded a corner and headed toward a church built of dark grey bricks. On top was a spire the same shade of bluish green as the Statue of Liberty. Perhaps it was made of copper. In science class, Mr. Garabini had said copper turned blue-green when it was exposed to air and water.

Analyn marched up the front steps and tried the door. Locked.

Vin sighed. "I knew I should have Googled the directions to get a better time estimation."

"C'mon." Nakia waved them to the far side of the building.

"Good idea, Nakia. Let's try another entrance." Analyn hurried after her while Vin nudged Kam and rolled his eyes.

"Actually, I'm trying the parish office."

Reluctantly, Kam and Vin followed the girls around the corner and along the side street. Behind the church was a red brick building. Etched into the glass door were the words "Oficina de San Procopio and Holy Trinity Croatian."

"Croatian?" Analyn raised an eyebrow. "I thought you said this was a Hispanic neighborhood."

"It is." Nakia marched up the steps and rang the bell. "But it used to be a Croatian neighborhood before that."

A middle-aged woman with thick, dark hair opened the door. "May I help you?"

"Hi, we're looking for someone who can tell us about St. Procopius."

The woman looked into each of their faces. "What exactly do you want to know?"

Analyn stepped forward. "Oh, you know, the usual. What he was known for. What's he the patron saint of? That kind of stuff."

"I'm not sure how much I can help with that."

Kam's heart sank. They'd come all this way—an hour and a half trip—and even the people at the church didn't know anything about St. Procopius. Immediately, Kam had visions of T.J. showing up at school with bags on top of bags of money.

A voice behind Kam broke his reverie. "Pardon me, children." A tall man with giant glasses and a rim of white hair eased his way up the steps.

"Deacon Donnelly," Nakia exclaimed. "Hello."

The old man blinked behind his glasses.

"It's me, Nakia. Remember? You baptized my little cousin Alfonso last month."

A grin brought out the wrinkles in the old man's face. *"Oh, sí, Señorita Nakia. Buenos días. ¿Cómo estás?"*

"Muy bien. ¿Y tú?"

Analyn leaned toward her brother. "He's asking how she's been, and she's telling him that she's very good."

"Yeah, I'm not a complete moron, Analyn. I do pay *some* attention in Spanish class." The tip of his gym shoe tapped the edge of the concrete step. Then he muttered, "I just don't have a great memory for vocabulary."

The old man bent slightly so he wouldn't tower quite so much over Nakia. "What can I do for you and your friends?"

Analyn stuck out her hand. "Hello, sir. I'm Analyn Cheng. This is my brother Arvin and his friend

Kameron. We're doing a school project on obscure saints."

Kam rolled his eyes at Vin. *Obscure* had been one of last week's vocabulary words, and Analyn loved to squeeze them into conversation any chance she got.

"We need some information on St. Procopius. Do you think you could help us out?"

"Well"—Deacon Donnelly rubbed what little was left of the white hair on the back of his head—"I've got another Baptism today. Why don't you follow me inside and we can talk while I set things up?"

Analyn beamed one of her Broadway smiles. "That would be perfect, sir." She nudged her brother. "Maybe we could also take some pictures of the church while we're inside." She smiled at the deacon again. "Our teachers really love multimedia presentations."

CHAPTER TWELVE

As Deacon Donnelly set out the holy oil—*chrism*, he called it—the candle, and the new garment for the infant, he repeated most of what Kam had read online about St. Procopius.

Analyn and Nakia listened with rapt attention while Kam followed Vin around as he took shots of the church's interior with his phone. He looked for any sign of what St. Procopius might be known for, but there wasn't even a statue of the saint in sight. He studied the stained glass windows and then looked up. On the arched ceiling were murals from the nativity: the birth of Jesus, the presentation at the temple, and the Archangel Gabriel appearing to Mary. A fourth mural puzzled Kam. A woman and a man knelt before a gentleman whose robes suggested he was a religious leader. Was the couple Joseph and Mary? The man looked like he was putting a ring on the woman's finger.

At the front of the church stood a tall, white marble altar with a matching crucifix at the top. In the arch above the altar, the words "Sancte Procopi Ora Pro Nobis" were painted in gold. To the right of the altar was a similar, smaller one surrounded by spring flowers in vases. Above the altar hung a gold-framed image of a woman wearing a blue robe with gold stars.

Kam slipped his phone out of his pocket, typed in a few words as if he were going to text someone, and then showed the phone to Nakia.

Who is she?

He pointed to the painting of the woman in blue.

"Our Lady of Guadalupe."

"Ah, yes." The deacon looked up from the baptismal font where he had laid out the holy water and oil. "She's one of our favorite depictions of Mary for the Latino community here at San Procopio."

Could Mary have anything to do with St. Procopius and who we're supposed to ask him to pray for? Kam couldn't imagine any connection there.

Suddenly, something the deacon said hit a familiar chord. He had called the church, "San Procopio," the same thing written on the front door of the parish office, but that wasn't what was written above the altar.

Kam reread the words painted along the arch. He pulled out his own phone and typed them into a search engine. For the first time that day, he had a glimmer of hope.

"Say," Deacon Donnelly said, as if a thought had just occurred to him, "what school did you say you were from? I know you don't go here."

The megawatt smile that had been plastered on Analyn's face suddenly fell away.

"It's not around here...exactly."

What if the Deacon began asking too many questions? Kam quickly typed out another message on his phone and shoved it in front of Analyn before she could say anymore.

I've got the answer. Let's go.

Analyn's eyes opened wide. "Oh, we've got to go."

"We do?" Nakia asked.

"Yep." She grabbed Nakia's arm. "Thanks, Deacon."

"Yes, thanks, Deacon Donnelly. Bye."

The deacon raised a hand. "I hope you got the information you need." He sounded a little disappointed.

Analyn shot him another smile as she grabbed Vin on the way out. "You were great. Thanks."

Outside, the spring breeze ruffled Kam's curls. He tried to smooth them down with one hand, but he knew without looking in a mirror that this was going to be one of those days in which his hair was uncontrollable.

"What's going on?" Vin shoved his phone in his pocket, but Kam gestured for him to take it back out.

"Kam's got the answer to the first riddle," Analyn said.

"I don't see how that's possible. The deacon didn't tell us anything new, and I didn't see much about old Saint Porcupine in that church."

Kam gave an impatient sigh and held his hand out for Vin's phone. He flipped through the pictures until he found a shot of the words above the altar. He showed it to Vin.

"Yeah, so? It's a bunch of words in a foreign language."

Kam pointed the phone toward Analyn.

"They look sort of like Spanish."

Nakia looked over her friend's shoulder. "You're close, but I'm pretty sure that's actually Latin. The two are similar." Then a smile spread across her face. "Good catch, Kam. You did solve the first riddle!"

CHAPTER THIRTEEN

"What?" Vin shrieked. "How?"

Kam held up his phone where the translation of *"Sancte Procopi Ora Pro Nobis"* still appeared.

The Cheng siblings elbowed each other to look at the phone first. Analyn read it aloud. "Saint Procopius, pray for us."

"That's it?" Vin said. "That seems too easy. We're just supposed to ask the saint to pray for us. All of us? Not a specific group?"

Kam shrugged. There was only one way to find out if it was right. He texted the Mystery Riddler.

The answer to the first riddle is "us."

Then for good measure, he added nobis to the end in case the Riddler wanted the answer in the original Latin.

"I think we should start for home," Vin said.

"I'm hungry." His sister rubbed her stomach.

"You're always hungry."

"I can't help it if I'm a year older and hit my growing spurt first."

Nakia tugged at Analyn's sleeve before World War III could start. "We passed a bakery on our way down Racine. We can get you a pastry and me a café con leche."

"A what?" Vin asked.

"Coffee with milk," Analyn translated.

As they headed off, Kam kept his phone in his hand. He didn't want to miss the Riddler's reply.

The bakery was a couple blocks away. By the time they arrived, Kam was worried the Riddler had decided to leave them without a second clue.

The four friends sat at a table, sipping their drinks and nibbling on churros and doughnuts. Kam was surprised at how little the food and drinks cost here. His mom never bought coffee at the shops in Winfield Park. It was way over-priced, but in this little family-owned bakery, even Kam could afford to buy a small doughnut.

From his window seat, Kam watched the people walking down the street. Three teenage girls walked by just as the door to the bakery opened. The three girls didn't enter, but their voices drifted in through the open doorway. They were talking excitedly, and Kam heard them mention Saint Procopius. He wondered if they were from the church, but their blonde hair and ivory skin didn't fit in with the Latino parishioners. Neither did their over-sized sunglasses or their huge handbags, which reminded him of the designer ones his mother eyed at the department stores.

Kam didn't have time to ponder the three girls for long. His phone buzzed in his pocket. Everyone looked toward him. He pulled it out of his pocket and held it up to show them.

Riddle #2: In the place where His name is sacred, what creature keeps company with a lion, an angel, and an eagle?

"Since 'His' is capitalized, we're talking about God." Nakia sat back in her chair to contemplate the riddle.

"So where is God's name sacred?" Analyn pulled at her one-sided ponytail. Again, Kam lamented that she couldn't split her hair into two even ponytails or at least wear the one ponytail in back. "Everywhere. His name is sacred everywhere."

Vin rolled his eyes. "But that doesn't tell us where to go. Obviously, we need to go somewhere again. Like to another church."

Analyn scrunched up her nose. "Sacred Name Church?"

Nakia shook her head. "I don't think there is such a place. I've heard of Sacred *Heart* Church."

As she smoothed down her long ponytail, Analyn's eyes suddenly lit up. "I got it. What's another word for 'sacred'?"

She held her hands open like she was waiting for them to shout out the answer at the same time.

"Holy," she proclaimed. "Don't you get it? We're going to..."

If there hadn't been adults in the bakery, Kam would've joined the other three in exclaiming, "Holy Name Cathedral!"

CHAPTER FOURTEEN

Before the cups and napkins were tossed in the garbage, Vin had the address for Holy Name Cathedral brought up on his phone. It meant taking the blue line back into the city, switching to the red line, and getting off at Chicago Avenue, just north of the Loop.

Despite the train transfers, Kam and his friends soon stood at the base of the cathedral's stairs.

In the understatement of the year, Nakia said, "This church is a bit bigger than the last one we were in."

With skyscrapers around them, the cathedral sat like a piece of medieval history plopped in the middle of a metropolis. But that didn't stop the seventh graders from craning their necks to admire the rose window above the main entrance or the spire that soared up to their right. Kam's right eye twitched. He squinted so that he could imagine the cathedral had a matching spire on the left. Why didn't the architects design these things more symmetrically?

The giant doors to the cathedral looked heavy, but they opened easily. After walking through the vestibule, the four friends entered the cathedral and gasped. The ceiling soared high above them. Wooden beams hinged by golden brackets arched from one flesh-toned marble column to another. Below them were more dark wooden pews than Kam had ever seen.

He let out a silent sigh. The outside of the church might be unbalanced, but the symmetry inside was beautiful.

Spread throughout the pews, a few people knelt in prayer. Nakia stepped up to a table in the back and picked up a parish bulletin.

"There's a noon Mass starting in a half hour," she whispered.

"We better look quickly," Vin replied. "What are we looking for again?"

"A lion, an eagle, and an angel." Analyn pointed to the right side of the church. "You two take that side. Nakia and I will take this one."

Kam and Vin headed up the right aisle, stopping to take pictures of the artwork along the way. In red frames were scenes from Jesus's life, which Kam soon recognized as the Stations of the Cross. No angels, lions, or eagles in any of them.

As Vin snapped a photo of Jesus falling for the first time, Kam looked back at the entrance. Above the glass doors was the largest organ he'd ever seen. His eyes followed the curve of the ceiling far above. In the center of the ceiling was a circle, and inside the circle were the letters, "ihs," but the "h" had a horizontal line across it so that it resembled a cross.

Around the circle were four smaller circles. Inside these were the names Matthew, Mark, Luke, and John, each accompanied a picture. Kam twisted his head to look at each picture in turn. He could feel Vin pulling up alongside him with his phone aimed to snap photos of the ceiling.

They both stopped and looked at each other. The pictures in the circles were the eagle, the lion, and the angel!

Without a word, they hurried across the church to where the two girls stood near the podium used for the Scripture readings.

"We've got the answer," Vin cried at the same time his sister declared the same thing.

"It's right here." Analyn pointed to the podium.

"No, it's right there." Vin pointed to the ceiling. "Look. An eagle, a lion, an angel, and..." Vin squinted at the last one. "A cow."

"It's an ox," his sister said, "and the answer's right here." She pointed to the bronze carving that made up the base of the podium. "See, the four men are Matthew, Mark, Luke, and John. Each of them has a symbolic creature, and Luke's is an ox."

"Are you sure that's not a cow?" Vin said.

"I'm sure." Analyn held up a pamphlet and pointed to a section entitled "Ambo of the Evangelists."

Kam read over Vin's shoulder.

The bronze artwork on the ambo depicts the four

writers of the Gospels. The angel represents Matthew, whose Gospel includes Jesus's genealogy or human side. The lion is a symbol for Mark who describes John the Baptist preaching like a lion roaring. John is represented by an eagle for his ability to see things at a higher level. Finally, Luke is represented as an ox because of his narration of Jesus's infancy.

Vin handed the pamphlet back. "Cow, ox, what's the difference? I didn't exactly grow up on a farm, you know."

An old woman in the first pew gave them the evil eye. Their voices were growing a bit too loud for a church. Kam gestured for his friends to follow him. As they walked down the long aisle, he texted the answer to the Riddler.

Once they were outside the church, Analyn said, "Now where?"

"We have to wait for the next riddle." Nakia took a seat on the steps of the church.

"Can't we at least start back home?" Vin brushed some dead leaves off a step before sitting down. Then he glanced at his hands and pulled out his antibacterial gel.

"We don't know where the next riddle is going to send us. Maybe west. Maybe back south."

"Please, not south again." Vin rubbed his hands together.

Kam pulled his backpack off and shoved his hoodie inside. The wind had died down, and the spring sun, noon-high in the sky, beat down on them.

When he looked up from zipping his bag closed, Kam spotted two familiar teenage boys walking up the steps. He nudged Vin.

Shading his eyes from the sun, Vin stared at their black clothes and piercings. He turned his gaze back to Kam. "From the train?"

Kam nodded. What would two teenage boys be doing going to church on a Saturday at noon?

"Other potential heirs?" Vin asked, his face scrunched up like he hoped he was wrong.

Kam shrugged.

The phone in his pocket buzzed, and the four friends gathered around.

Riddle #3: In the place where you'll hear Spanish instead of Croatian, which rarely depicted sacramental event takes a high spot?

"Spanish instead of Croatian?" Analyn read the words aloud.

Vin groaned. "Oh no, we're going back to St. Porcupine's, aren't we?"

CHAPTER FIFTEEN

A gruff voice called from the base of the church stairs. "Well, Marc, look what's going on here—a real, live dorkfest."

T.J. and Marc laughed as they climbed two stairs at a time.

"What are you losers doing here?"

Kam clutched the yo-yo in his left pocket and held tightly onto the phone in his right.

Analyn was quickest with an answer. "We're sight-seeing downtown." She folded her arms and gave them a smirk.

T.J. laughed. "Only dweebs like you would think visiting a church was sight-seeing."

Analyn was undaunted. "What are *you* doing here then?"

T.J.'s face fell. He wasn't as quick with making up excuses.

Gorilla-sized Marc opened his mouth. "We're gonna get our hands on..."

T.J. elbowed him. "Shush it, man." He turned back to Analyn. "None of your business." He turned toward the church. "C'mon. We've got business to attend to."

T.J. and his bodyguard headed into Holy Name.

As soon as the door shut behind them, Analyn said, "No doubt about it. They're after the same treasure we are." She sighed. "We better get going."

Kam shook his head.

"You're not giving up, are you?" From a few steps below, Nakia looked up with big brown eyes.

A steady stream of people now headed into the church for noon Mass. Kam's throat felt tight. He shook his head before pointing to his phone and then Vin.

Vin scratched his head for a moment, then his eyes lit up. "Kam, you're a genius. We don't have to go back to St. Porcupine's. I took photos of the place with my phone."

"Oh, Arvin, that's perfect," Analyn exclaimed. "That'll put us way ahead of T.J. For once, Arvin, I'm actually glad you're my brother."

"I'd believe that if you remembered to call me *Vin!*" He pulled out his phone and scrolled through the pictures.

"Kam," Nakia said, "let me see the riddle again."

Kam showed her the text, and Nakia read it aloud. "'Which rarely depicted sacramental event takes a high spot?' Okay, look at pictures that were placed either high up or at the front of the church."

"A sacramental event," Analyn repeated the words to herself. "There are seven sacraments: Baptism, Reconciliation, Eucharist, Confirmation, Matrimony, Holy Orders, and..."

"Last Rites or Anointing of the Sick," Nakia finished the list.

"Right."

"What about this one?" Vin stopped on the mural in which Mary and Joseph bring the infant Jesus to the Temple. "It's sorta like a Baptism."

"I don't think so," Nakia said. "It's called the Presentation at the Temple. I've seen paintings of that before. The clue said the event was 'rarely depicted.' We've got to look for a sacrament that isn't often shown in pictures."

Vin scrolled to the next photo.

"Annunciation." Nakia identified it.

Vin scrolled again.

"Birth of Jesus." Analyn called the next one.

Vin continued until Kam grabbed his arm.

"What?" Vin said.

Kam waved his hand to indicate Vin should go back one.

"What's that supposed to be a painting of?" Vin asked.

"The woman in blue must be Mary," Analyn said.

"And the man across from her has to be Joseph. Who's the old, bearded guy in the middle?"

Kam typed a word on his phone and pushed it in front of Vin's.

"Wedding," Analyn read the text aloud. "Of course, it's Mary and Joseph's wedding. It works. Matrimony is a

sacrament. I can't remember any time I've seen a painting of Mary's and Joseph's wedding."

"Text it quick, Kam," Vin said. "We don't want to be
here when T.J. and Marc come out."

As Kam texted the answer Matrimony, Analyn waved a
hand at Vin. "Ah, those two brainiacs will take all day to
figure out the answer."

Streams of tourists strolled past the church. Some entered the church. Others walked down the busy city sidewalk, weighed down with multiple shopping bags.

Suddenly, Kam got the feeling he was being watched.
A man sitting at a bus stop across the street yanked a
newspaper in front of his face. Over the edge of the
printed page, Kam could see a brown newsboy cap. Could
it be one of the old men from the train? But then, where
was the other old man?

Kam was about to tap Vin on the shoulder when a
voice behind him caught his attention.

"Still here, huh, losers?" T.J. strode down the stairs,
Marc laughing behind him. "Don't do too much exciting
sight-seeing in one day."

A black limo pulled in front of the church in time for
T.J. and Marc to hop in. Kam wondered whose dad owned
the limo, T.J.'s or Marc's. Both of them could afford it.

"How did they finish so fast?" Vin cried.

"They must have gotten help from someone," Analyn
said.

As the limo drove off, Kam's gaze fell on the bus stop
across the street. The man with the newspaper was gone.

CHAPTER SIXTEEN

Kam's phone buzzed in his pocket. The message read:

Be more specific.

"What?" Analyn wailed. "We don't have time for this. We texted the sacrament. What else does this guy want?"

"It could be a woman who's texting him," Vin said. "Based on how picky the person's being, I'd bet it *is* a woman."

"When it comes to being picky, Arvin, you live in a glass house."

Nakia stepped between the siblings. "Kam, text back 'Mary and Joseph's wedding.' That should be specific enough."

Kam did as Nakia suggested while Vin decided to take pictures of the cathedral's exterior.

Within moments, Kam's phone buzzed again.

Riddle #4: In the church where Polish once reigned but Latin is now the order of the day, what tool comes before the spear and the sponge?

As Vin pulled out his phone and began typing the words "Polish church in Chicago," Analyn talked through the problem out loud.

"We need a Polish neighborhood in Chicago. Great." Sarcasm dripped from her tongue.

"The only city that has more Polish people than Chicago is Warsaw," Vin said without looking up from the search engine on his phone.

"Exactly my point. This could be any of dozens of churches in the city."

Kam pulled the yo-yo from his pocket, flipped it up and down a few times, and then let it sleep. They had to get to the next church before T.J. and Marc, but how could they figure out which one it was?

"You're forgetting the next part of the clue," Nakia said. "Latin is now the order of the day. Not too many churches still say Mass in Latin. Not since Vatican II, as my grandfather keeps reminding me."

She had a point. Kam pulled his yo-yo into an "around the world" before putting it back in his pocket and spying over Vin's shoulder.

"I think I got it."

The girls pulled up on either side of Vin.

"Look. St. John Cantius Church does the..." Vin paused to figure out the next word on the parish's website. "Tried-un-tine?"

"Tridentine," Nakia corrected him, pronouncing the word like "try-den-teen."

"What she said," continued Vin. "Latin Mass. It says here the Masses are like the ones before Vatican II."

"Is it in a Polish neighborhood?"

"Yep." Vin tapped another section of the screen. "Says here, 'Founded by Polish immigrants at the end of the nineteenth century.'"

"So where is it?" Analyn leaned over her brother's shoulder.

Vin tapped a few more instructions into his phone. "Not too far. According to this map, it's basically straight down Chicago Avenue, which is..."

"That way." Nakia pointed toward the subway exit they had taken, and the four headed down the stairs of Holy Name Cathedral.

"Are we taking a train again?" Vin whined.

"No," Nakia said, "there isn't an 'L' line that goes that way."

"Good."

"Is it close enough to walk?" Analyn asked.

Vin consulted his phone again. "Looks like it's a mile and a half. That means a half-hour walk, at least."

"We don't have time." Analyn pulled at her ponytail. "T.J. and Marc were in a limo."

"Then we'll have to take the next best thing," Nakia said. "The bus."

Vin sighed. "I'm gonna need more hand gel."

CHAPTER SEVENTEEN

Kam's silent prayer for a bus to arrive quickly was answered, and the foursome hopped on a #66. Vin kept his hands in his pockets so as not to touch anything.

Weekend traffic forced the bus to crawl through the skyscraper-lined street, but Kam kept reminding himself it was faster than walking. Perhaps not faster than cycling, though, as he watched a cyclist speed past the bus.

When they hopped off, Vin pointed the way. The exterior of St. John Cantius looked like an ancient Greek building. Above the three open doors were tall Greek columns and a triangle with the words "Ad Majorem Dei Gloriam." Kam typed the words into a search engine to reveal their meaning. Why not? Translating Latin had worked for the first riddle. Besides, he was trying to ignore the fact that this church had a bell tower on the right and no matching one on the left. Was there no respect for symmetry in the architecture of this city?

As Kam pecked away on his phone and climbed the steps to St. John Cantius, Analyn and Nakia discussed where a spear and a sponge might be hidden in a church.

"Did I hear you talking about the spear and the sponge?"

Three blonde teenage girls wearing ridiculously large sunglasses stood at the church's entrance. They were the same ones Kam saw pass the bakery back in the Pilsen neighborhood. The girl in the middle wore a purple hoodie that matched her sunglasses. She took them off and eyed the two girls and then the boys.

"So I heard there was a mystery cousin participating in Great Uncle Edward's little game. Which one of you is it?"

Although the girls were only a few years older than Kam, something about them made them intimidating. Maybe it was their height because they were tall enough to be Wonder Woman's Amazon cousins, or maybe it was their model-perfect appearances.

Analyn, Nakia, and Vin immediately pointed to Kam, whose eyes grew wide. How could his friends rat him out?

"Ah." The girl smiled, reaching forward to ruffle Kam's red curls. "So you're my long lost cousin. How are the riddles coming, coz?"

Kam didn't need any adults in the vicinity to make his throat tighten.

"Not sharing any secrets, huh?" She winked at him. "How many more riddles do you have left?"

"We're nearly halfway done," Vin bragged.

Why did his best friend have such a need to be the smartest person in the room?

"Really?" the blonde said. "We've only got three left." She studied Vin, taking in his smart phone and his button-down shirt tucked into his jeans. She snatched the phone from his hands. "Is your list of riddles on here?"

"Hey," Vin squealed.

"Relax, I'll give it back. I only want to see if we've got the same ones." She held up a piece of paper she'd pulled from her massive handbag.

Analyn tore the phone from the girl. "Our list of riddles isn't in there."

"Wait." Vin eyed the sheet in the blonde's hand. "Do you already have *all* the riddles?"

The blonde laughed. "Of course, don't you?"

The looks exchanged between Kam and his friends were enough to give the girl her answer. Inside, Kam boiled. Why was the Mystery Riddler feeding them the clues one at a time? T.J. probably had the full list, too. That meant less time heading back and forth. They could have mapped out all the churches ahead of time and then plotted the fastest route between them.

"Oh, I see. That really does make things hard for you." The blonde smiled. "What would you say to a little alliance?" The two girls behind her stepped forward as if to speak, but the lead blonde held up a hand.

"Why would we form an alliance with you?" Vin asked.

"Oh, I don't know," the blonde began. "Maybe because Cousin T.J.'s last text said he had only two riddles left, and that makes him our common enemy."

Kam pulled out his yo-yo and dribbled it up and down. T.J. had only two riddles left, and they still had four to go. He felt the future of St. Jude's slipping away from him.

"What do you propose?" Vin asked.

The blonde eyed her sheet of riddles. "We're having trouble with riddle #2. You guys figure out what church that is?"

All four of them nodded.

"Good." The girl smiled. "You give us the answer to riddle #2 so we don't have to make the trip, and we'll give you the answer to riddle #6."

"That seems like a fair trade," Vin said.

"Hold it," Analyn said. "Give us a minute to discuss." She grabbed her brother's arm and waved Nakia and Kam down the church steps. After they'd huddled, Analyn whispered, "I don't trust those girls. How do we know they'll give us the right answer?"

"We don't." Vin's answer surprised Kam. A moment ago, he seemed ready to take the blonde's offer. "We give them the wrong answer and hope they give us the right one."

Nakia shook her head. "Lie to them?"

"We'll tell them the answer is a cow, like I first thought it was."

Analyn turned to Kam. "It's your fortune to lose, Kam. What do you think? Do we trust them?"

Kam popped his head out of the huddle. Behind him, the three blondes fiddled with their phones. With their huge sunglasses, their facial expressions were hard to read. A quick scan up and down the street revealed no other people in the vicinity.

Poking his head back into the huddle, Kam whispered, "Let's trade only the names of the churches. That way, they still have to travel all the way to Holy Name."

Vin sounded disappointed, but Nakia and Analyn liked the plan.

"Okay." Analyn faced the three blondes. "We'll trade you the name of the church for riddle #2 if you tell us the name of the church for #5."

The head blonde scrunched up her nose for a bit. The blonde to her right leaned over and whispered something in her ear.

"Fine," the blonde said. "We'll take your deal, although we're wasting time. T.J.'s gonna beat us, and I can't stand to hear the little greaseball gloat. What's the church for riddle #2?"

"Holy Name Cathedral." Analyn crossed her arms. "Now what's the church for riddle #5?"

"St. Stanislaus."

The blonde to her left flinched.

"Great." The head blonde gave Kam's curls another playful pat. "You seem too nice to be a cousin of mine. Tell ya what. Here's a freebie. The answer to #4 might be 'crowns.'" She bounded down the steps. "May the smartest heir win!"

CHAPTER EIGHTEEN

As soon as the blonde teenagers left, Analyn cleared her throat. "I still don't trust them. Riddle #4 asks for a tool. Crowns aren't tools."

"Let's head inside." Nakia led the way through the open doors.

St. John Cantius Church was larger than St. Procopius but smaller than the cathedral. However, that didn't make its appearance any less impressive. In fact, its coloring was similar to the cathedral. The pews were a golden brown wood, and the marble columns that supported the roof bore shades of brown and gold. The half dome over the altar was painted a deep gold with murals of several saints and angels. The large altar had columns similar to the ones outside, but they were dark brown instead of stone gray.

The only person in the church was a dark-skinned man wearing a long black robe.

"Monk?" Analyn nudged Nakia, who shook her head.

"I don't think so." Nakia kept her voice low to match her friend's reverent tone.

Vin pointed to the floor. "Analyn, is this what Mom meant when she said we'd get inlaid wood floors if we were rich?"

Kam worked hard not to shake his head in front of his friends. Didn't the Chengs know they *were* rich? A lesson from Mr. Garabini's science class floated into his memory—something about Einstein's theory of relativity.

Analyn examined the floor. Dark wood pieces sat between pieces of lighter colored wood forming patterns on the floor. "Yeah, Mom would love this," she said.

The four friends walked up the main aisle. The light-colored wood pieces gave way to a dark-rimmed square. Inside the square was a lighter-colored circle, and inside the circle was a six-pointed star. At the center was a capital letter P with an X over it. In religion class, Mrs. Harris had said this was a symbol for Jesus.

A bit further down the aisle was another dark square. Inside this one were three crowns. The four friends exchanged glances. Maybe the blondes hadn't lied to them after all.

As if reading Kam's thoughts, Analyn whispered, "Crowns still aren't tools."

They ventured onward. The next dark square had an X in the middle. The top left point of the X resembled an arrow. The top right point ended in an octagon. Three small T's were placed directly to the left, top, and right of the X's center. Shooting down the center of the X was a straight line that ended in a rectangle.

Analyn, Kam, and Vin looked to Nakia for an explanation. She shrugged.

The next dark square was easier to decipher—a cross with a banner flying over it. Clearly, a reference to Christ's crucifixion.

The final square, at the end of the main aisle, had a star with—Kam counted silently—eight points.

"Admiring our inlaid floors?" The man in the black robe had slipped behind them. He spoke with a bit of an accent that reminded Kam of the African missionary priest who'd visited St. Jude's a couple months ago. He sounded almost British, but not quite. The edge of a white collar could be seen around his neck.

Analyn's flashed him her megawatt smile. "Yes, we are, Father...?"

The man's head inclined slightly. "I'm not a priest yet. I'm a seminarian. It's a beautiful floor, isn't it? Wonderful how the designer wove the story of Christ's life into the floor."

"What do you mean?"

The seminarian pointed toward the first dark square. "The life of Christ starts down there with his birth represented by the Star of David, and it ends here." He pointed to the floor below them. "This eight-sided star represents the final coming of Christ."

Kam scratched his head.

"Oh, I get it," Nakia said. "The three crowns represent the three kings for the Epiphany, right?"

The seminarian smiled. "Yes. Some also say they represent the three ministries of Christ—prophet, priest, and king."

"And this one"—Nakia walked to the cross and the banner—"is His death."

"Actually, that's His Resurrection. The banner over the cross represents the Resurrectionist Order of Priests." The seminarian smiled. "I'm studying to join their order." He followed Nakia down the main aisle.

"So then this one in the middle must be His death."

"Correct."

Kam stared at the design again, trying to make sense out of it.

"But it's an X, not a cross," Analyn said.

"Look again. See what's at the end of these lines?" He pointed with his fingers.

"That one looks like an arrow," Analyn said.

"Not an arrow." Vin's eyes lit up. "A spear."

"And that one's a sponge." Analyn pointed to the line with the octagon on its end. "The blondes were telling the truth. Look, the crowns come before the spear and the sponge."

"Do you know the three young ladies who were here?" The seminarian raised his eyebrows.

"Not really," Nakia said.

"You see, Father...I mean..." Analyn faltered.

"Call me Brother Rob." The seminarian smiled.

"You see, Brother Rob," Analyn continued, "we're in the middle of this scavenger hunt, and we're trying to find a tool that comes before the spear and the sponge."

Brother Rob scrunched his nose. "Crowns aren't really tools."

"That's why I think the blondes are wrong," Analyn said.

Suddenly, a grin split Brother Rob's face. "Come look at the spear and the sponge from this angle." He gestured for the children to stand on the altar side of the square so that the spear and sponge were upside down. "Now what else do you see?"

"Three upside-down T's," Vin said. "Oh, they're the three nails."

"Nails aren't tools either." Nakia shook her head.

"No," Vin said, "but a hammer's a tool, and you need a hammer to use the nails."

Vin knelt on the floor and pointed to the long line that ended in a rectangle.

"Yes," Brother Rob said. "I think you've found your answer."

"Of course," Analyn said. "The soldiers used the hammer to crucify Jesus before they offered the wine on the sponge and before they stabbed His side with the spear. So they literally used the hammer before the spear and the sponge. *And* as you walk up the aisle, you step over the hammer before the spear and the sponge."

Kam checked his watch, prompting Vin to do the same.

"It's after one o'clock," Vin said. "We better get going. We've got three more riddles to solve."

CHAPTER NINETEEN

After thanking Brother Rob, the four headed out of St. John Cantius. Kam texted the answer as they walked down the church steps. Vin pulled up the map function on his phone.

"How do you spell St. Stan-is-slaw? Oh, never mind. It popped up after the first few letters."

"Is it far?" Analyn peered over his shoulder. "I'm getting hungry."

"You're always hungry."

"I could use another café con leche." Nakia scanned the short block that housed St. John Cantius.

"St. Stanislaus Kostka is about a mile from here." Vin looked up from his phone. "The directions say to head down Chicago Avenue and then turn right onto Milwaukee."

"But we haven't received the next riddle yet," Analyn warned. "Those girls could've lied about the church."

"True, but if we walk this way, maybe we'll find you some lunch."

"Oh." Analyn's eyes widened. "Good plan, Arvin."

Her brother sighed, and the gang headed back to Chicago Avenue. The walk to Milwaukee Avenue was short, and they soon turned right, searching for a restaurant. They passed a cell phone store, a hair stylist, several dry cleaners, numerous brick factory buildings, and a few new condo buildings.

"Where's a McDonald's when you need one?" Analyn groaned.

They came to a long bridge that crossed over an expressway.

"Which road is this?" Analyn asked.

Vin consulted the map on his phone. "Kennedy Expressway."

Kam recognized the name. If he followed it north, part of it would split off to the Edens Expressway, which would bring him home.

Cars zoomed below them. Kam followed their path down the road, part of him wishing he were in one of those cars. Somewhere, way north of here, his mom and Gram sat home safe in suburbia and had no idea he and his buddies were walking the streets of Chicago.

On the far side of the bridge was a large brick building with a gigantic red-and-white sign that read "National Headquarters Polish Roman Catholic Union of America." Not too surprising. They'd just left a Polish church and, with a name like Stanislaus, it sounded like they were headed to another one.

"This way." Vin pointed down a side street with old apartment buildings.

"Are you sure?" His sister eyed the older buildings. The apartment complex looked deserted.

"That's what the directions say."

"Let me see." She snatched the phone from her brother. "Let's stick to the main streets—Milwaukee to Division. I'd feel safer. Besides, there's a better chance of food this way." She handed back the phone and marched forward.

"You and your food."

A few minutes later, Analyn spotted a place that sold sub sandwiches. Kam didn't want to admit it, but he was glad Analyn had insisted they head this way. His stomach was growling, too.

They ordered their food and then took the sandwiches to one of the few open tables in the front. Bread crumbs and broken chips were scattered across the table and plastic chairs.

Vin reached inside his pocket. "Sometimes, I think there's not enough hand gel in the world."

Despite Vin's complaints about Analyn always needing food, the four children devoured their sandwiches. As Kam polished off a ham and cheese sub, his phone buzzed.

Riddle #5: In the place where His name is sacred, what one word sums up Matthew, Mark, Luke, and John?

After reading the text silently to himself, Kam typed a few words in a new message and showed them to his friends.

The blondes lied.

CHAPTER TWENTY

"We're supposed to be headed back to Holy Name, not St. Stanislaus." Analyn slumped back in her seat. "I knew we shouldn't have trusted them."

"We came all this way for nothing," Vin sighed.

"At least we got food."

"Yeah, but we have to head all the way back to Holy Name, and we've just moved farther from it." Vin slapped his forehead. "When we gave them the church for #2, we were also giving them the church for #5."

Kam felt ill. Not only had they not received the right church name, they'd helped the blondes with two of the riddles!

Nakia leaned forward in her seat. "Maybe we don't have to go all the way back to Holy Name. We solved the second St. Procopius riddle without going back. Let's think about the riddle for a moment. What one word sums up Matthew, Mark, Luke, and John? They're all Gospel writers, but that's two words."

"Maybe the answer's just 'writers,'" Vin suggested.

"Or authors?" Analyn twisted her ponytail around her finger.

Kam typed a word on his phone.

Apostles?

"No." Nakia shook her head. "John and Matthew were, but Luke and Mark weren't. Analyn, do you still have that brochure from the church? The one that listed the symbol for each Gospel writer?"

Analyn rummaged through her tote bag. "Here it is." From Kam's angle, he could see the pamphlet had photos and descriptions of the artwork in the cathedral.

Nakia looked over Analyn's shoulder.

"Got it," the two girls exclaimed at once. They placed the brochure on the table for the boys to see, then pointed to a paragraph titled, "The Ambo of the Evangelists." Beside it was a picture of the podium with the metal carvings of the four writers with their creature symbols.

Kam pointed to the word "Ambo" and raised an eyebrow.

"No," Nakia said. "Ambo means the podium. You want 'evangelists,' that's the word for the Gospel writers. I'm kind of surprised I didn't think of it before. Must be the lack of caffeine. I wish they had café con leche here." With that, Nakia got up to refill her cup at the soda fountain.

After texting his answer, Kam looked out the window. Two boys skateboarded past. A family eating ice cream cones strolled the other way. For a moment, Kam thought the skateboarders would collide with the youngest boy who was so busy licking the drippings off his cone that he didn't see the oncoming traffic.

A ways down the street, nearly out of Kam's line of vision, was a bus stop, the kind with a bench inside a glass shelter. Kam squinted. Two old men in flat caps and beige trench coats sat on the bench, partially hidden by the advertisement on the side of the shelter.

Inside the restaurant, two adults sat at the table next to them. No way Kam could talk now. He nudged Vin and pointed to the men.

"What?" Vin said.

Kam pointed vigorously. Vin had to lean over to see that far down the street.

"What are you pointing at? The bus stop?"

Kam nodded.

"What about it?"

Kam tapped away on his phone and then showed it to Vin who read it aloud. "They're following us!"

"Who?" Analyn turned around and craned her neck to look in the direction Kam pointed. "Who's following us? Those old men?"

"What's going on?" Nakia slid back into her chair with her filled cup.

"Those men." Analyn pointed. "They're following us."

"Are you sure?" Vin turned to Kam.

Kam nodded.

Nakia studied the men for a bit. "Are they the same ones who jumped on the train at the last minute back in Winfield Park?"

Kam nodded again.

"Yeah, I thought I saw them near Holy Name, too."

"What do you think they want?" Analyn tugged nervously at her ponytail.

"I don't know," her brother said, "but we've got to ditch them."

Kam's phone buzzed on the table. All eyes fell on it. He hit the button to read the text.

Riddle #6: In the place where Eucharistic adoration is a 24/7 business, what color is sorrow?

Immediately, Vin typed "Eucharistic adoration 24/7" into a search engine.

"All I'm getting are explanations of what Eucharistic adoration is and churches in other cities." Vin scrolled through the list. "Boston, Cleveland, Albany."

"Maybe we should try answering the question without finding the church. I mean, isn't blue a logical color for sorrow? You know, like when you're feeling blue."

Kam thought it was worth a try. He texted the word blue to the Mystery Riddler.

"Wait a minute," Vin said. "Where would those blondes have come up with the name St. Stanislaus?" He tapped more words into his search engine. "Here it is. They didn't give us the church for riddle #5. They gave us the church for #6! I knew they weren't smart enough to come up with another church name that quickly. See?" Vin showed them the results on his phone. "St. Stanislaus Kostka is open twenty-four hours, seven days a week, for people to come in and pray."

"See, Arvin? It's a good thing we listened to my stomach and headed this way after all." Analyn grinned.

Vin smirked. "Let's get going."

"What about the old men?"

The four friends craned their necks to check on their followers. They were still seated at the bus stop.

"What are we going to do?" Nakia said.

Analyn grinned. "The same thing they do in movies. C'mon. Follow me."

CHAPTER TWENTY-ONE

The couple at the next table threw away their wrappers and headed out. The sub shop was now empty except for the four friends and the teenage boy manning the counter. He was whistling softly as the four approached. With no customers to wait on, he entertained himself by placing a quarter on his upturned elbow and then flipping his arm down to catch the quarter in his hand.

"Excuse me." Analyn used her sweetest voice. "Do you happen to have a back exit?"

The boy dropped the quarter. "Ah man, I was going for a record—fifteen in a row."

"Sorry. We didn't mean to break your record."

The boy's pimply face reminded Kam of a pepperoni pizza. "That's okay. Miguel's way better than me anyway. He can do a whole stack of quarters on his elbow and catch them all with one hand. What was it you wanted?"

"A back exit. Do you have one?"

"Of course we got one. Gotta have it for safety reasons. You know, fire codes and stuff. Plus, it's where I take out the trash."

"Do you think we could use it?"

"Ah, the boss man doesn't like strangers back by the kitchen. You know, health codes and stuff."

"We wouldn't touch anything in the kitchen. We just need to get out of here, you know..." Analyn lowered her voice. "*Unnoticed.*"

Pimple Face bent toward Analyn and imitated her voice. "*Unnoticed?*"

"Yeah." Analyn kept her voice low. "We've got some old guys following us." She pointed over her shoulder toward the window.

The boy grinned. "What, are you like some spy kids?" He gave a short, nervous laugh. "Like in those movies."

Vin crossed his arms. "Listen, buddy, it's a matter of national security. Do you really want to be responsible for the downfall of civilization as we know it?"

The boy stopped laughing. Vin could look pretty serious in his button-down shirt. "Why didn't you say so in the first place? C'mon." He waved with his hand. "The boss man's out on lunch break. He'll never know."

He led the four past a small kitchen with a large sink. Beyond it was a door with a red "EXIT" sign. It opened before the teenage boy could push the metal bar.

On the other side of the door, a burly man wiped a hand on his grease-stained t-shirt. "Roger!" the man yelled. "What are these kids doing...?"

"Run, kids, run," Pimple Face screamed, pushing the four kids past the burly man.

Kam and company didn't hesitate. They skittered around the man, who stood with his hand holding the door open and his mouth gaping.

"This way." Vin pointed down the narrow alley behind the row of shops. They took off, running.

"Save the world!" Pimple Face shouted.

"Thanks," Analyn yelled back.

They could hear the burly man yelling at Pimple Face behind them, but they kept their eyes on the end of the alley ahead.

When they came out on the main street, Analyn asked, "Where are we?"

"Division Street," Vin pointed to a street sign, "which means St. Stanislaus should be a couple blocks this way and then a left on Noble."

A few minutes later, they turned the corner around a gas station.

"That must be the church spire up ahead." Nakia pointed to a dark tower a block or two ahead.

Kam winced as they drew closer to the church. The building had two towers, but only the left one had the complete spire. It was as if the bell portion of the right tower had been knocked right off. *So close to being symmetrical.* Kam sighed.

"Get down." Vin grabbed Kam's arm and tugged him behind a parked car.

"What?" Analyn asked.

"Down. Now!" Vin's voice was a harsh whisper. With a wave of his hand, he indicated they should get down next to the car.

The girls obeyed.

"What are we hiding from?" Analyn whispered.

"The limo—didn't you see it?"

Analyn shook her head.

"It's pulled up in front of the church. It's T.J.'s, I'm sure. The license plate says, 'TJR 3.' You know, for his dad, Theodore Jefferson Reynolds, III."

"So what do we do now? Wait here until they leave?"

"Do you want to run into T.J. inside? If he sees us at a second church, he'll know one of us is the 'mystery cousin' as the blonde called us."

"Yeah, but if we wait, he'll be one clue ahead of us." Analyn tugged at her ponytail. "Let's at least get a little closer to the church so we can get in as quickly as possible after he leaves."

Nakia peered over the roof of the car next to them. The church was on the other side of the street, about ten car lengths away. Nakia ducked back down. "There are several cars parked along the street here. Let's inch over one by one." Nakia took one last peak over the roof, then waved to the other three.

They took off down the sidewalk, keeping low. After catching her breath, Analyn peeked through the window of a beige sedan. "Go." They edged over to the next car.

At the fourth car, Kam took his turn checking before they ran. He ducked back down almost immediately and put a finger to his lips. From the other side of the car came the deep voice of a boy who'd hit puberty early.

"How many more of these museums do we need to visit?"

"Hang in there, Marcs-man. We've only got one more. Holy Trinity."

The slam of a car door followed. Moments later, they could hear it taking off down the street.

Vin stretched his neck to see over the hood of the minivan they hid behind. "Move," he yelled, and they sprinted across the street.

CHAPTER TWENTY-TWO

"Whoa!" A man seated at a table inside the church doors held up his right hand. "Where are you four going in such a hurry?" The man was seated, but his broad shoulders and long legs sticking out from under the rickety table made it clear he would tower over any of the St. Jude's kids.

Analyn shot him her Broadway smile. "We're here for the Eucharistic adoration."

The man humphed. "I'm not falling for that one again." He straightened some of the books for sale on the table. Kam noticed a box for donations to the man's left.

"What do you mean?" Analyn asked, her voice all innocence.

"A couple boys just left here. Said they came for the Eucharistic adoration, too, but all they did was run around the church. Rather disrespectful to the others trying to pray."

Nakia stepped forward. "To be honest, sir, we're here as part of a scavenger hunt."

"Church ain't no place for kids to be playing."

"What's the donation box for?" Analyn pointed.

The man glanced at the small box to his left before answering. "This church is old. They've done a lot of restoration, but there's still much to do."

"What if we made a donation?" Analyn asked. "Then could we go in?"

"Young lady, you can't bribe your way into a church. This is a sacred place. It's open to all who want to come and worship our Lord. All we ask is you do so quietly and reverently."

"Oh, we can be quiet and reverent," Analyn responded, perhaps a bit too enthusiastically to be believable. "In fact, Kam over here doesn't talk at all in front of strangers." She pointed to Kam, who nodded hurriedly in agreement.

"Is that so?" The man turned his attention to Kam. "You don't talk at all?"

Kam shook his head.

"Does that mean you can't talk, or you do talk?"

Kam nodded, then stopped. Then shook his head. Was he saying yes, he couldn't talk, or no, he could talk?

Thankfully, Vin stepped up. "He *can* talk, just not around adults when he's outside his house."

"Oh, I see," the man said, but his expression made it clear he didn't. "Listen, I can let you in the church if you all promise to be prayerful."

Analyn gave a little hop and clap of her hands.

"But," the man warned, "if I hear one squeal or one giggle or anything that disrupts the others who are praying, I'll have to ask you to leave immediately."

"We'll be good." Analyn held her hand up like she was giving a Scout's honor.

"All right then." The man nodded, and the four stepped inside.

The inside of St. Stanislaus was bright and airy, despite a scaffolding on one side where a wall was being painted. Creamy-colored columns held up arches on either side of the main seating area. In the center, above these arches, a vaulted ceiling painted in gold and blue soared three stories over their heads. On either side of the church, beyond the columns, was more seating under vaulted ceilings only two stories high. Bright stained-glass windows lit up the space. As Kam walked up the center aisle, he noticed the windows were spaced so that they sat evenly between the marble columns. The windows' rounded tops matched the curve of the arches between the columns.

Nakia poked him in the arm and pointed toward the right side of the church. In front of a series of pews was an unusual statue. It was of a woman dressed in red robes who sat in a position that reminded Kam of the yoga poses Gram did. Her hands rested on her knees with her palms open toward him. In the center of her chest was a large circular opening. From this distance, Kam couldn't tell what was in the center other than something pale in color. On either side of the red-robed woman were two golden angels, kneeling in prayer, their giant wings curving upward in an arc toward the head of the woman.

Kam felt himself drawn toward the statue. The others must have felt the same way, for the four of them soon stood before the statue in awe.

"What is it?" Analyn whispered.

"I have an idea," Nakia whispered back, "but I'm not sure. I'll tell you when we leave."

"Does it have anything to do with our clue?" Vin used his hand to cover his mouth and keep his voice low.

"I don't think so," Nakia said.

Kam pulled out his phone and reread the riddle.

Riddle #6: In the place where Eucharistic adoration is a 24/7 business, what color is sorrow?

He agreed with Nakia. The statue of the woman in red didn't have anything to do with the color of sorrow. Kam headed to his right, and Vin followed. Without saying a word, the girls headed in the opposite direction.

The afternoon sunlight sparkled through the stained glass windows. One window depicted Mary kneeling before Jesus as he placed a crown on her head. Another showed her on a cloud while two people knelt at her feet. They were beautiful windows with bright colors and intricate details. Each image was framed by a set of stained-glass columns and surrounded by white scrolling on a yellow background. Below each image was a stained-glass bouquet of yellow roses.

Kam continued down the side aisle. The next window depicted Mary surrounded by men. He counted the men. The twelve apostles, he concluded. They each had a tongue of flame above their heads.

The following few windows showed Jesus instead of Mary. One was clearly Jesus's ascension into heaven. Another must have been His resurrection. He was wrapped in a white garment, and an angel knelt as His feet. After that, Jesus was shown on the cross with His mother and an apostle at His side. Then a window of Jesus carrying the cross, stopping in front of a woman in blue who had to be Mary.

Kam felt like the windows were walking him backwards through Jesus's life. The next window showed the crowning with thorns.

Having reached the end of the stained-glass windows on this side of the church, Kam turned toward the other side when a glance at the stained-glass roses stopped him. The roses below the crowning with thorns were red. In fact, as he looked back, the last three windows all had red roses under them while the first five windows had yellow.

Kam hurried to the other side of the church.

Windows depicting Jesus being whipped and Jesus praying in a garden had red roses. But on the third window on this side, the roses changed color again. A scene of Jesus as a boy standing before a worried Mary and Joseph had white roses underneath. The same with the next four windows. Kam took note of the scenes in each window: an elderly man holding the infant Jesus while Mary and Joseph stood nearby, Mary and Joseph with the baby Jesus as shepherds watched, an older woman in red kneeling before a pregnant Mary, and Mary being visited by an angel. All of the last five windows had white roses depicted under the image.

The answer to the riddle was there, on the tip of his tongue—if only he could talk it out with someone.

CHAPTER TWENTY-THREE

Kam couldn't talk in the church. Several adults were kneeling in prayer. Vin took photos of the stained glass windows. Not far from the altar, Analyn and Nakia studied an image of Mary with the baby Jesus.

Kam hurried to the girls and tapped Nakia on the shoulder. When she turned around, he waved his hand for her to follow him.

"Did you figure it out?" she whispered.

Kam nodded.

Analyn turned around and whispered, "What's the answer?"

Kam jerked his head toward the exit and headed down the aisle. On his way out the church, he grabbed Vin by the arm.

"I'm not done with photos," Vin stage whispered.

Kam didn't care. On the way through the vestibule, he stopped at the man sitting by the table.

"Did you find what you're looking for?" the man asked.

Kam nodded, then dug into his pocket and pulled out a few dollar bills. He placed them in the donation box.

The man's eyes grew wide. "Well, thank you, young man. That's real nice of you."

Kam nodded again. He didn't look back as he exited the building, but he had a feeling one or two of his friends followed his example.

Outside, Kam scanned the street. Two cars passed by, and a kid rode his bicycle down the sidewalk. Across the street was a park. Not much there other than an empty ball field and a grassy area. Fortunately, no one was playing a game at the time.

After another car drove past, Kam crossed the street and headed to the park. A black iron fence surrounded it, so he had to walk a ways to find an entrance.

"Kam, wait up," Analyn called behind him. "Where are you going?"

Kam headed to an open area in the middle of the park. Except for the occasional car passing by and the distant hum of the expressway on the other side of the church, the place was quiet. Kam plopped himself down on the over-grown grass.

"Okay," Vin huffed as the others caught up to Kam and joined him in a circle in the park's center. "There's no one else around, so talk. What's going on? Did you figure out the riddle or what?"

Kam cleared his throat. "I think I've got it."

"That's great," Analyn beamed. "What color is it?"

"I've got it narrowed down to three: yellow, red, or white."

Analyn scrunched her nose. "None of those seem like 'sorrow' colors to me. What makes you think it's one of those?"

"The stained glass windows." Kam's voice came out a little easier now, but he was still barely audible. "Did you look at the pictures in them? They reminded me a bit of the Stations of the Cross, but the scenes didn't quite match up. I mean, some of them did—Jesus's death, the crowning with thorns, but some of them were on His early life—His birth, His baptism. And then some of them were more about Mary than Jesus—the Archangel Gabriel visiting her, Mary visiting Elizabeth."

"What's that have to do with the three colors?" Nakia asked.

Kam pointed to the right side of the church. "The first five of the windows on that side had yellow roses pictured under them. Then," Kam did a mental count of the windows, "three of them had red roses. On the other side of the church, the first two windows had red roses, but the next five had white roses."

While Kam talked, Vin flipped through the photos on his phone. He stopped suddenly and said, "So there were five of each? Five yellow, five red, and five white?"

"Yes." Kam rubbed his chin. He had heard this trio of fives before. A memory floated back to him. He was sitting at home and Mrs. Harris had come to visit him. It was the night she showed Kam how she always kept a rosary in her pocket to keep her calm when she worried.

"I've got it!" Kam's words came out so much louder than normal that his friends all jumped. "The mysteries of the rosary. Mrs. Harris taught me about them. First, you have the five joyful mysteries. They would include Mary visiting Elizabeth and the birth of Jesus. Then there are the five sorrowful mysteries, all about Jesus's death. And finally the five glorious mysteries—you know, Jesus's rising from the dead and all that. Don't you get it? The sorrowful mysteries. What color is sorrow?"

Nakia sat up straighter. "Red."

Analyn finished her thought. "Because the windows that depicted those mysteries had red roses under them."

Vin flipped through his photos to confirm the idea while Kam texted the answer.

Analyn peered over Vin's shoulder. "Stop flipping through the photos, Arvin. Start looking up Holy Trinity. That's what T.J. said was the last church, and somehow, we've got to beat him there."

CHAPTER TWENTY-FOUR

"We might have a little problem here," Vin said after typing "Holy Trinity Church" into his search engine. "There seems to be more than one Holy Trinity in Chicago. There's one in Hyde Park, one downtown, one on the west side, one on the north side."

Before Vin could read off any more, Kam's phone buzzed.

Riddle #7: In the noble place where the Father, Son, and Holy Spirit combine, to which country does the Holy Family flee?

"Well," Analyn said, "at least we know T.J. had the right answer when he said, 'Holy Trinity.' That name certainly fits with the Father, Son, and Holy Spirit."

"Yeah, but we still don't know *which* Holy Trinity Church we're supposed to visit," Vin said.

Nakia ran her hand over the long grass. "Maybe it doesn't matter."

Three pairs of eyes stared at her.

"Maybe we can answer the question without going to any of the Holy Trinity Churches. The riddle is pretty straightforward. Where did the Holy Family flee?"

Three faces scrunched in concentration.

Nakia continued, "There's only one story of Mary, Jesus, and Joseph fleeing that I know, and it happened shortly after Jesus was born."

"Egypt," four voices cried in the park.

Kam texted the word, then looked up at his friends. "What if T.J.'s already texted the answer?"

"T.J. probably didn't think of the answer that fast," Vin said.

"What if the blondes finished first?" Kam said.

"Impossible." Analyn smoothed her dark ponytail.

Kam had one more fear. "What if we get the treasure, but it's not enough to save St. Jude's?"

The four friends fell silent.

Kam played with a wide blade of grass between his fingers. In the distance, an ambulance siren blared. When it died down, Kam could once again hear the cars whizzing down the expressway on the other side of St. Stanislaus.

"My mom said," Nakia spoke, her voice even quieter than usual, "if St. Jude's closes, I'll have to go to a Catholic school in the city. My aunt knows of one whose tuition isn't too high, and she can drop me off there before work."

Analyn undid her ponytail and then redid it. "Our parents said they don't know where they'll send me and Vin, but there's been talk of a boarding school in Wisconsin."

"What about you, Kam?" Vin looked at his friend. "Where will you go if St. Jude closes?"

Kam shrugged, even though he really knew the answer. "Might go back to my old school."

Vin squinted. "The one that wanted to put you in special ed?"

Kam lifted one shoulder in a half shrug.

"You should come with us," Analyn said.

"Yeah, maybe." Kam kept his eyes cast toward the single blade of grass he now squeezed between his thumb and forefinger. There was no way his mom and Gram could afford the tuition at a boarding school—even a Catholic school in the city like the one Nakia would go to was out of the question.

Kam's phone buzzed.

"This is it," Analyn sat up on her knees. "We'll know if we won or not."

"You mean if *Kam* won or not," Vin corrected.

Analyn playfully punched him in the arm. "Oooh, you know what I mean. Hurry up, Kam, read the message. Let's find out if we're sticking together at St. Jude's."

Kam took a deep breath and tapped the button to read his message.

CHAPTER TWENTY-FIVE

Please wait where you are for further instructions.

"What?" Analyn cried. "What's that supposed to mean? Did we win or not? I mean, did *you* win or not?"

"I don't know," Kam confessed. "Maybe there are instructions for retrieving the treasure." He stuck his phone in his pocket and leaned back on the grass.

Vin's phone rang.

"Who's calling?" Analyn asked.

Vin checked the caller ID. His eyes widened. "It's Mom."

"Don't answer it. You've never been good at keeping secrets from Mom."

Vin glared at her but let the call go to voicemail.

Restless, Kam stood up. He pulled his yo-yo out of his pocket and, after a few warm-ups, began doing around-the-worlds and rock-the-cradles. As he continued, he picked up the pace, spinning the yo-yo faster and faster, and whipping it around with such velocity that Vin felt the need to duck-and-cover at one point. But Vin needn't have bothered. Kam had the yo-yo under perfect control. The only purpose for his speed was to try to make time go faster.

When Vin's phone buzzed to let him know he had a message, he listened to his voice mail. Kam stopped spinning the yo-yo and watched as Vin's face grew pale.

"What did Mom say?" Analyn asked.

"This isn't good. She wants us home early for dinner. She and Dad are meeting the Meyers for a seven o'clock movie, so she wants us home by five."

Kam checked his watch. It was already 2:30, and getting home would take at least an hour.

"Maybe I should call her back," Vin said.

"No." Analyn shook her head. "We're almost done. Just wait a bit longer."

As if on cue, Kam's phone buzzed again. Everyone gathered around as he read the message.

> To find the treasure, you must seek it deep within the church. You might say it lies within the body of Christ.

"Oh, my gosh," Analyn breathed. "This is it. If we solve this last riddle, we've done it."

"But what does it mean?" Vin scratched his head.

"It says, 'deep within the Church,'" Kam said. "Do you think that means we're supposed to look inside the basement of Holy Trinity? You know, like it's buried treasure underneath the church or something?"

Nakia's forehead wrinkled. "Maybe. The previous message did say to wait right where we were, and he probably thought we were in Holy Trinity when we texted the last answer."

"But we still don't know which Holy Trinity." Analyn threw her hands up. "We don't have time to run around from church to church. T.J.'s going to beat us!"

Vin had his phone out again. "Kam, read the seventh riddle to me again, the one about Holy Trinity and the whole fleeing thing."

Kam scrolled to the seventh riddle. "In the noble place where the Father, Son, and Holy Spirit combine, to which country does the Holy Family flee?" He looked up from his phone. "Does that help?"

Vin held up one finger in a "wait" sign while he tapped his phone with the other hand. In a moment, he smiled. "Didn't you find it kinda funny that he called it a 'noble' place? Remember the name of the street we're on? Noble." Vin pointed to a street sign and then turned around his phone to show them a map he had pulled up. "And there's a Holy Trinity Polish Mission Church on Noble Street a couple blocks south of here."

"Arvin, you're a genius," credited Analyn.

"Yes, I am. And as a genius, I think you should respect me by calling me Vin!"

"Oh stop arguing, you two." Nakia was the closest to exasperated Kam had ever seen her. "We've got a treasure to find.

CHAPTER TWENTY-SIX

The walk down Noble Street wasn't long at all. It was amazing to imagine a time when two churches were needed so close together.

As they crossed over Division Street, Analyn yelled out, "Look, a wedding." Both she and Nakia gasped. Vin and Kam exchanged looks and then rolled their eyes. What was it about girls and weddings?

Analyn and Nakia sprinted ahead toward the guests gathered in front of the long white limo. Women in fancy dresses and men in suits blew bubbles at the bride and groom as they descended the church steps. By the time Vin and Kam caught up, Analyn and Nakia were cheering with the guests as the limo drove off.

A few feet away, a middle-aged woman with a professional-looking camera snapped photos. An elderly gentleman walked up to her and asked, "Aren't you doing any photos inside the church?" He had a flower in the lapel of his tux.

The photographer looked up from her camera after snapping one last shot of the retreating limo. "Yes, they wanted to do the bubbles first so the guests didn't have to wait. The limo's going to turn around and come right back."

Vin nudged his sister who was still waving good-bye to the limo. "Let's get inside and find a way to the basement before they come back inside to take photos."

"Good idea," Analyn said, but she moved reluctantly toward the church, her eyes following the limo down the street.

For the first time, Kam got a good look at Holy Trinity. It reminded him a bit of St. John Cantius. The entrance had four gray stone columns topped by a triangle. However, one major difference made Kam fall in love with this church immediately. It had two—yes, two—bell towers. One on the right and one on the left. Perfect symmetry!

Above the arches, yet below the triangle, the words *"Kościół Trójcy Świętej"* were written in gold. Kam hoped the words meant "Holy Trinity Church" because typing *"Kościół Trójcy Świętej"* into an online translator seemed impossible.

The doors into the church's interior were open, and a few wedding guests mingled around, discussing how to get to the reception. One of them raised an eyebrow at the children with their jeans and gym shoes. Inside the church vestibule, Analyn pulled the little group to the side.

"What?" Vin asked his sister.

"T.J. and Marc are inside," Analyn whispered.

Kam peered around the open doorway to see for himself.

"Don't look," Analyn admonished, but Kam couldn't help himself. The church captivated him. It felt more open than any of the previous ones because it didn't have huge columns in the middle supporting the roof. And then there was all the color. The back altar was huge and nestled into a large alcove. Although the back altar was mostly gold and white, it had colorful statues and murals painted on it and above it.

On either side of the sanctuary were two smaller altars, miniature versions of the main one. Above each of these was a circular stained glass window in shades of blue and red. The symmetry of it all thrilled Kam. If only the whole world were laid out in such order!

And then there was the ceiling, beautifully divided into rectangular sections with the most colorful murals imaginable. The walls were no less bold. Tall, narrow stained glass windows joined three-dimensional depictions of the Stations of the Cross. In the center of the left wall was a raised area. Two sets of stairs led up to the platform. In the middle of the stairs was an open area, in which a gold rail curved downward. A set of stairs that led to the basement, perhaps?

Kam was about to check for a matching platform and set of stairs on the opposite side when he felt a tug pulling him backwards.

"Get back here." Analyn pulled Kam away from the open door just as he spotted T.J. and Marc near the small left altar. "We need to find a way to the church basement without T.J. or Marc spotting us."

Kam nodded and pointed to himself.

"You know a way downstairs?" Vin asked.

He nodded again.

"How?" Nakia asked.

Kam crept back to the open doorway. T.J. and Marc had moved to the raised platform on the left side of the church. They were busy studying some of the artwork. A quick peak to the other side confirmed Kam's suspicion that the right side of the church also had a raised platform. If he were right, the curved golden railing between the platform's two sets of stairs would lead downstairs.

Checking once more to make sure T.J. and Marc weren't looking their way, Kam motioned for the others to follow him as he eased into the church. He kept his body low and crouched behind the pews. Analyn, Nakia, and Vin did the same.

"Now what?" Nakia whispered.

Kam pointed to the right. They would have to crawl along to keep out of T.J.'s sight, but as long as they stayed on the opposite side, T.J. shouldn't see them.

It felt ridiculous to be crawling along the floor of a church, but Kam hoped God would know it was all for a good reason. Surely, God would understand his desire to keep his school open. He hadn't thought much about God before moving in with Gram. Mom wasn't all that religious, but Gram always talked about how Jesus could understand all our concerns because He had been human, too. At first, Kam thought that was all a bunch of nonsense. How could anyone who lived two thousand years ago understand his problems today?

But Gram also said that God was someone we could turn to in our times of need, and if ever Kam had need of some extra help, it was now.

Halfway to the sets of stairs, Kam's knees ached from sliding across the wooden floors. The church was so quiet. Only a few sounds from the wedding party outside drifted in. Were T.J. and Marc still on the raised platform or had they moved on?

Finally, they reached the stairs. The golden railing led down half a flight of stairs to a landing. Here, the stairs turned and divided into two separate flights.

Kam pointed toward the stairs, and all three of his friends gave him a thumbs up. He couldn't continue to crawl, so Kam raised himself into a low crouch and headed down. The others followed suit.

He made it to the landing and was about to turn right when a voice called across the church.

"Hey," Marc yelled. "Isn't that Dork Face and his friends?" He pointed from the raised platform directly opposite them.

Like deer caught in headlights, Kam and company froze on the stairs, all of them in a crouched position and staring back at T.J. and Marc.

T.J. locked eyes with Kam. Then he whacked Marc's arm. "One of them's the mystery cousin."

"Go!" Vin yelled.

CHAPTER TWENTY-SEVEN

Vin's command was hardly necessary. The four leapt up from their crouched positions and flew down the stairs. Kam and Vin to the right, Analyn and Nakia to the left. Kam hoped that by splitting up they'd confuse T.J. and Marc, but when he reached the base of the stairs, he saw that the other stairs had led the girls to the exact same room: a linoleum-floored basement the same size as the church above and supported by thick beams.

"This way," Nakia whispered.

The basement was only partially underground, so some natural light came through small windows near the ceiling, allowing them to maneuver around the many folding tables and chairs. The room looked like a church hall and was probably used for large gatherings and meetings. Nakia led them behind a series of boxes and paint cans piled up in a corner. Once they'd settled in, she pulled a large drop cloth over their heads.

Seconds later, heavy footsteps could be heard pounding down the stairs.

"Where'd they go?" The deep voice could only belong to Marc.

"They must be hiding," T.J. said.

Gym shoes squeaked on the linoleum floor.

In a loud voice, T.J. called, "Hey, dorks, you can't hide in here forever." His voice echoed slightly in the cavernous basement.

Kam's heart pounded in his chest. He couldn't believe they were hiding in a church basement. What would they do if T.J. found them? Maybe T.J. would give up if he didn't find them right away. Persistence wasn't exactly a stellar quality for T.J.

"You're not gonna find that treasure before me," he called, "so you might as well give up now. I don't care which one of you thinks he's my cousin—the family treasure doesn't belong to you. Uncle Edward was crazy when he wrote up that will."

Despite the darkness underneath the drop cloth, Kam knew his friends were looking at him. His stomach churned. He had no idea who Uncle Edward was, or what exactly his will said, or why he was involved at all. All he knew was the treasure was his only chance for saving St. Jude's and keeping his friends together.

The squeaking of shoes became louder. *They're headed our way!* Kam bit his tongue.

"Who's down there?" a woman's voice called.

The shoes stopped squeaking. High heels could be heard clicking down the stairs.

"Who are you?"

There was a pause before T.J. responded. "We're looking for some friends."

"I didn't ask what you were *doing."* The edge in the woman's voice reminded Kam of Mrs. Harris when she reprimanded T.J. for talking in class. "I asked who you *were."*

"Friends of the groom?" Marc offered.

Kam imagined T.J. punching Marc in the arm for sounding stupid.

"All right, that's enough," the woman said. "You two get out of here."

"But our friends..." T.J. insisted.

"Are clearly not hanging out in the church basement," finished the woman. "Now get out of here."

The squeaky footsteps started up again, then faded away.

The woman gave a loud humph and then muttered something about children playing in churches. Moments later, her high heels could be heard clicking toward the stairs.

Vin's phone buzzed. The woman's high heels stopped. Had she heard? A rustling sound told Kam his friend was hurrying to silence his phone. He held his breath.

Seconds passed. No one made a sound.

After an eternity, the woman's heels could be heard once again, clicking their way out of the basement.

When they had faded far in the distance, Analyn peaked over the cloth. "Coast is clear," she said.

Slowly, the others emerged. Vin took out his phone. He headed toward one of the small windows to read his message.

"Uh oh," he said.

"What?" Analyn hurried to his side.

"Mom texted that she went to Kam's house and no one's home. She's wondering where we are."

"You've got to text back something," Analyn said. "You know Mom. If she doesn't hear from us soon, she'll call the police."

"What do I say?"

"Text her that we went to do some research for our project and that we'll be home by five. We're almost finished here."

"We better be," Vin muttered as he sent off the message.

Placing her hands on her hips, Analyn surveyed the church basement. A doorway opposite them was labeled "Kitchen," and a slightly raised platform on the one end looked like it could have been used as a stage.

"Now where?" Analyn asked.

Kam reread the final clue.

To find the treasure, you must seek it deep within the church. You might say it lies within the body of Christ.

Well, they were as deep within the church as they could go, but what did the second sentence mean?

Kam nudged Vin. "The body of Christ?"

"I have no idea what that means," Vin said. "It's not like they've got Christ's body buried down here."

"Or do they?" Nakia walked toward the stairs.

"Huh?" Analyn asked. "You're the last person I'd expect to say that, Nakia. Remember the whole resurrection thing?"

"Oh, I don't mean they actually have His body down here, but look." Nakia pointed to a sign that read "Crypt" with an arrow pointing toward a door.

"Crypt?" Analyn scrunched her nose. "Like where they bury people?"

Nakia nodded and slowly opened the door. It creaked as the four peered into a dark tunnel.

"Something tells me this door is normally locked," Vin said.

"C'mon, let's see what's inside." Analyn stepped in and flipped a nearby light switch. The yellowish tunnel walls were so narrow they could barely walk two by two. The passage curved through a winding path. The walls were monotonous except for the occasional niche that held a gold statue reminiscent of a trophy. They had round bases, narrow pedestals like candlesticks, and large sunbursts on top. In the center of each sunburst were tiny pieces that looked almost like rocks or teeth. Under each niche was a sign with a name. Kam read one silently as he passed. "Sw. Jozafat."

"It's like the catacombs in Paris and Rome," Nakia whispered. A sense of awe kept them hushed.

"The cata-what?" Vin asked.

"Catacombs," Nakia repeated. "It's where they used to bury people underground."

Kam shivered at the thought. The narrow tunnel was feeling smaller by the moment.

After several curves, they reached a dark area that branched off. Analyn felt her way along and then flipped another light switch. She gasped. Kam, Vin, and Nakia followed quickly behind her.

"They did bury Christ down here!"

CHAPTER TWENTY-EIGHT

Kam couldn't believe his eyes. The small side branch of the tunnel led to a tiny cave, or at least that's how he perceived it. On the back wall of the miniature cave, an artist had painted gray stones that curved, creating the illusion of two, small arches. The arch to the right framed a mural of the soldiers guarding Christ's tomb. In the smaller arch to the left, an angel played the violin. But the most astonishing part was what lay on the bench before the arches—a statue of Jesus wrapped in a white shroud pulled up to his chin, his face turned toward the children while a light shone from above.

"Holy…" Vin began.

"Don't even say it," his sister warned.

"This has got to be one of the weirdest and yet coolest things I've ever seen," Kam breathed. His friends turned to look at him. "What? There aren't any adults around. I can talk."

They all nodded and went back to looking at the crypt, but secretly, Kam was a little surprised at himself for being able to speak out loud in a situation this weird. How often did you find a statue of the deceased Jesus awaiting resurrection tucked into a catacomb beneath a church?

"The treasure must be here." Analyn scrutinized their surroundings. "The instructions said to look within the body of Christ."

"Oh, no way," Vin said. "We are not breaking open a statue of Jesus."

Something clicked, and the room went dark.

"What just happened?" Analyn cried.

An evil laugh echoed through the catacombs.

"T.J." Vin whispered, identifying the laugh.

Kam bit his tongue. To be so close and have T.J. spoil everything was unendurable.

"Quick, find the light switch near the entrance," Analyn instructed.

Kam could feel his friends brush past him in the dark, but he headed the opposite way. He was glad he couldn't see what his hands were doing as they groped around the shroud encasing the statue of Jesus. He didn't want to have Jesus looking at him while he was pilfering his tomb, even if it was only a statue in a fake grave. Not feeling anything unusual near Jesus's feet, Kam slid his hand along the far side of the statue, working his way up toward the violin-playing angel. That's when he felt it— something hard under the shroud, not much longer than his forearm, and moveable, definitely separate from the statue.

T.J.'s laugh echoed through the dark tunnel again. "So you thought you could hide in here, did ya?"

Kam moved his hands under the shroud and clasped the rough-shaped object. In the dark, his fingers felt something smooth, like sanded wood, and something thin and slick like a piece of wire.

T.J.'s voice grew louder. "Marc and I have the two entrances to the tunnel covered, so you're going to hand over the treasure whether you like it not."

Kam fumbled while opening his backpack and stashing the object inside. As he let it go, his fingers brushed something that felt like paper and—was that tape?

"What are we going to do?" Analyn whispered.

"Tell him the truth," Nakia said. Then she called loudly, "We don't have it."

"Yeah, right," T.J. called. By the sound of his voice, he wasn't standing too far away. "Why don't you come out and hand it over."

After slipping his backpack on his shoulders, Kam reached for the yo-yo in his pocket.

"How can we come out?" Analyn said. "We can't even see where we're going."

"Hey, Marcs-man," T.J. yelled. "Turn on the lights."

The sudden bright light blinded them. When Kam's eyes adjusted, he saw T.J. standing at the entrance to the grave, and he heard footsteps coming toward them.

"So where is it?"

"We told you. We don't know." Analyn rested her hands on her hips.

Marc's huge frame filled the entrance to the grave. "Dude, did you get it? Whoa, is that like a dead Jesus or something?" Marc's height allowed him to see over everyone's heads to the statue behind them.

Kam pulled Vin to the side so Marc could get a good look. If the statue could distract them long enough...

T.J.'s eyes fell on the scene within the cave. "Dude." He drew closer. Analyn and Nakia edged the opposite way, making room for both T.J. and Marc. The tiny grave was overcrowded, to say the least. "That's gotta be the weirdest thing I've ever seen in a church."

Kam pulled the yo-yo out of his pocket and threw a few practice drops.

Suddenly, T.J. turned around and noticed the four inching towards the exit. "Hey, where do you think you're going?"

"We give up," Vin said. "The treasure's all yours." Analyn shot him a look. She clearly was not ready to give up.

"So where is it?"

Vin shrugged. "Somewhere with Jesus?"

T.J. and Marc both leaned over the statue. "Where?"

In one easy motion, Kam threw his yo-yo in a backwards around-the-world, aiming it perfectly for the light switch at the grave's entrance, throwing them into the pitch dark. With the blackness surrounding them, he found the courage to yell, "Run!"

He took off down the tunnel to the right, using his hands to guide him. A few quick turns brought him to the light of the church basement. Glancing over his shoulder to make sure his friends were behind him, Kam ran to the stairs. Up and around he ran, his friends clomping up the stairs behind him.

Upstairs in the main church, the bride and groom were having their picture taken in front of the altar. Groomsmen in tuxes and bridesmaids in bright green dresses milled around. Kam took off down the side aisle and headed for the exit.

As he pushed through the doors, he took a swift look behind him. T.J. and Marc were scrambling down the aisle, not ten feet behind Analyn.

An old woman was waving her purse at them. "Children. Children, stop running."

Kam knew he shouldn't have run in the church, but he couldn't let T.J. see what he had in his bag. He pushed open the door to the outside steps and nearly fell over. Standing right in front of him were the two old men with the flat caps and the beige trench coats.

CHAPTER TWENTY-NINE

The two old men stood with their backs to him. A quick cut to the left and Kam was flying down the stairs past them.

"Excuse us," Vin cried as he barreled down the stairs.

"Pardon me," Nakia called.

Kam racked his brain for a plan. How could he get them away from T.J. and Marc, not to mention the two old men?

A cry behind him caused him to turn around. It sounded like someone falling. Correction—two people falling.

T.J. was sprawled on the church steps directly in front of the old men. Marc lay beside him with one leg on top of T.J.'s as if he'd tripped over him. One of the old men poked his cane against T.J.'s back.

"Watch where you're going, sonny." The old man punctuated each word with a tap of his cane. His voice was unusually high for an old man.

Kam and company didn't wait to see what happened next. They zoomed past the limo waiting for T.J. and Marc and bolted down Noble Street toward Division. Not far away, a bus pulled to a stop.

"Jump on," Analyn yelled from the rear.

No encouragement was necessary. Kam hopped on, inserted his card, and fell into the nearest empty seat. The others followed suit. By the time Analyn boarded the bus, T.J. was turning the corner onto Division with Marc chugging behind him. Kam prayed the bus would pull away fast.

The bus driver closed the door just as T.J. ran up and pounded on the glass. The bus driver opened the door again.

"You're cutting it close," the driver said.

T.J. ignored him and boarded the bus, heading straight toward Kam.

"Where do you think you're going?" the driver barked. "You's got to pay to ride the bus."

"Pay the man, Marc," T.J. said.

Marc stood near the fare box and pulled a bill out of his wallet. "All I've got is a hundred."

Despite his fear of being stuck on a bus with T.J., Kam rolled his eyes. Oh to have the problems of the rich!

"We don't give change," the bus driver said, "and we certainly don't take hundreds. Why don't you get yourselves a taxi?"

"Why would I take a taxi when I've got a limo waiting for me?" T.J. said.

"A limo?" The bus driver threw the bus into park and stood up. He was far taller than he had appeared when seated. The top of his head nearly reached the bus ceiling. "All right, that's enough. I don't allow no monkey business on my bus. You two boys get off."

"But..." T.J. pointed toward Kam and Vin.

"Now," the driver demanded.

T.J. and Marc scuttled off the bus, but not before T.J. yelled back, "You better not have that treasure."

The bus driver threw a warning glance toward Kam and Vin as if to say, *You better not cause any trouble either.*

As the bus pulled away, Kam watched T.J. and Marc through the dirty window. They lumbered their way back to Holy Trinity. T.J. looked up as the bus passed. When he caught Kam watching him, he responded with a rude hand gesture.

Kam looked away.

Analyn tapped him on the shoulder. She and Nakia sat in the seat behind the boys. "What are we going to do now? T.J. and Marc will figure out the clue and break open that statue."

Kam couldn't help but smile. His friends had no idea he had pulled the treasure out from behind the statue while the catacombs were dark.

"What?" Vin furrowed his eyebrows at Kam's unexpected smile.

While Analyn and Nakia peered over the back of the seat, Kam unzipped his backpack. The bus rumbled over a pothole. Carefully, Kam lifted the object out of the bag. He'd finally see the object his hands had fumbled with in the dark.

Based on the odd shape and wooden feel, he wasn't too surprised when the object turned out to be a statue. However, he was surprised by what it was a statue of.

"What are you doing with a statue of a shepherd boy?" Analyn asked.

Kam ran his fingers over the shape of the statue. The young shepherd boy had one sheep slung across his shoulders and another rested at his feet. In his hand was the thin metal staff Kam had felt in the dark.

Vin's eyes widened. "Did you take that from...?"

Kam nodded his head back in the direction of the church.

"No way," breathed Vin.

"Do you mean *that*"—Analyn pointed to the shepherd boy—"was in the tomb?" Her mouth hung open for a second. She lowered her voice. "With Jesus?"

Kam nodded again. An elderly woman across the aisle was eyeing the statue in his hands.

Nakia reached over the edge of the bus seat and ran a finger along the shepherd's crook. "So this is the treasure?" she asked.

"Maybe it's super valuable," Analyn said. "Like one of those things you see on that antiques show Grandpa watches on PBS."

"It looks like it belongs to a Nativity set," Nakia said.

Kam remembered feeling something other than wood and metal when he'd picked the statue up. He turned the shepherd boy over. A small, folded piece of paper had been taped to its back. Carefully, he peeled it off and unfolded the paper.

Nakia read the typewritten note aloud. "Please return me to my home – St. Jude Parish, Winfield Park, IL."

CHAPTER THIRTY

"You did it," Analyn cried. "You found the treasure!"

"Hold on," her brother said. "This could all be a coincidence. After all, the paper doesn't say, 'Congratulations, you found the treasure.' Kam, text that guy and tell him what you found."

Kam did as he suggested.

Found statue of shepherd boy. Believe it's the treasure. What now?

"What if it's not the treasure?" Nakia asked.

Analyn shrugged. "At least Kam can return it to St. Jude's. Obviously, it belongs there."

The bus came to a stop, and several new passengers boarded. Kam slid the statue back into his backpack. Better to keep it safe and out of sight. He kept his phone in his hand, ready to read any response from the Mystery Riddler.

While they waited, they discussed what they thought the shepherd boy might be worth. Or at least three of them discussed what it might be worth. Kam kept his eye on the woman across the aisle who kept looking at them.

His phone buzzed. Four pairs of eyes read the screen at the same time.

Treasure must be verified by lawyer. Meet Mr. Wallerby at St. Jude Church after school on Monday.

"Monday?" Analyn whined. "We have to wait until Monday to find out if we're right?" She grabbed Kam's phone and shook it like she was yelling at it. "Can't your Mystery Riddler tell us if you've got the right object or not?"

Kam snatched the phone back. Analyn could be so impatient sometimes. Actually, he wished the Riddler had told him that much as well, but he figured wills meant lawyers, and he'd have to deal with them.

"At least T.J. didn't get his hands on the statue," Nakia said.

"True." Analyn sank back in her seat. "I wish it were all over. The school meeting is Wednesday. We don't have much time."

—

Worried the statue might break, Kam wrapped it in tissue paper he borrowed from Gram's gift-wrapping supply box. He kept the statue in his backpack for the rest of the weekend. Neither Gram nor his mom had said anything when he returned home in time for dinner Saturday night. In fact, only Mom was home when he arrived.

When she asked how the riddles were going, Kam replied, "I've got a good start. I'll know better on Monday."

After dinner, he turned on the computer in the den and looked up the lawyer, Mr. Wallerby. He was a little worried the whole thing might still be a joke, but Mr. Wallerby had his own website on which he stated that he specialized in wills and business contracts. Websites could be faked, but it all seemed pretty legit.

By the time Mass ended Sunday morning, Kam was itching for Monday to arrive. To distract himself, he spent Sunday afternoon researching famous people for his oral report for Mrs. Harris, but no one caught his interest. Everyone famous was talented or super smart. They had done wonderful things, and they were—how could he put it?—way more normal than he was. Their throats didn't close up at the thought of speaking in front of others. Many of them were, in fact, known for giving great speeches. Abe Lincoln. John F. Kennedy. No, he couldn't relate to any of them.

At school on Monday, Kam was careful about the way he unpacked his books, making sure no one spotted the tissue-wrapped statue. St. Jude's didn't have lockers, so students kept their backpacks and coats stuffed into a large closet in the back of the room. Kam worried about leaving the statue there as he moved from class to class, but no one except his three friends even knew it was there so he figured it was safe.

At recess, the four friends found their usual quiet spot. It was a windy spring day, and Kam wrapped his windbreaker tighter around him as the breeze picked up.

"What time are you meeting the lawyer?" Vin asked.

"The message said after school. You're coming, aren't you?"

Vin exchanged looks with his sister. They both looked worried.

"We can't." Analyn picked at a pebble on the ground. "Mom told us this morning we have orthodontist appointments right after school."

Kam looked to Nakia.

"Sorry. My mom's picking me up right after school, too."

"You're leaving me alone with the lawyer? How am I supposed to talk with him?"

"Why don't you use your white board like you do with Mrs. Harris?" Vin suggested.

"Mrs. Harris understands about my talking. The lawyer will think I'm a freak." Kam bit his tongue.

His friends fell silent.

Kam pulled his yo-yo out of his pocket and began doing tricks. The up-and-down motion helped to clear his head. He'd have to use his whiteboard as Vin suggested. The lawyer might think he was crazy, but there was no way around it. He had to save St. Jude's. He couldn't go back to his old school where the teachers thought he was stupid and the bullies made T.J. look like Miss Congeniality.

A loud cry echoed over the playground. T.J. was lying on the ground and holding his knee. A recess monitor ran up to him.

Kam and his friends couldn't hear what was said between them, but T.J. was soon limping off the playground. The recess monitor guided him in the direction of the school office where Mrs. Sullivan doubled as both the school secretary and nurse.

"What's wrong with *him*?" Vin asked, as if T.J. had no right to get hurt and require medical attention.

"Who cares?" Analyn said.

"Analyn." Nakia, the moral compass, poked her. "That's not nice."

"Yeah, well, did you see that hand gesture he gave Kam the other day? *That* wasn't nice."

"Yeah," Kam added, "and that's nothing compared to what he did to my dad's old yo-yo."

"I was wondering why you were carrying that new one around," Analyn said.

Kam told them all the story of how T.J. had broken his prized possession. The group consensus was that they were more certain than ever that T.J. didn't deserve to be the heir to Great Uncle Edward's treasure. Not that any of them had a clue who Great Uncle Edward was.

Before long, the bell rang and they were headed back into school. Kam hung his windbreaker in the giant closet, squeezing his backpack to feel the tissue-wrapped statue inside.

He froze. Where was the statue? He picked up the bag. It felt much too light. He unzipped it and looked inside. The statue was gone.

CHAPTER THIRTY-ONE

Kam felt around the inside of his bag as if the statue could have crawled into a corner. No. There was no doubt about it. The statue was missing.

His stomach clenched. He looked around the classroom. Most of the seventh graders had already headed across the hall to science.

Kam hurried after them and slipped into his usual desk next to Vin. He pulled out his whiteboard and wrote, "It's gone."

Vin raised his eyebrows. "The statue?"

Kam nodded.

Mr. Garabini flipped off the classroom lights and turned on the projector. "Okay, everyone." He pointed to the screen. "Let's see how you did on the homework."

Around the room, students pulled out worksheets on the human digestive system, but that didn't stop Vin from whispering, "How? Who?"

After pulling out his own homework, Kam scribbled on his whiteboard. "T.J. must have snuck into room after seeing Mrs. Sullivan about his 'injury.'"

Positioning the whiteboard so Vin could read it, Kam watched the expression on his friend's face. He could practically see the gears turning in Vin's head. His friend was smart enough to figure it out. Somehow, T.J. learned he had the treasure and then faked an injury at recess so he could sneak inside and rummage through his bag.

"What are you going to do?"

"Do you have a question, Mr. Cheng?" Mr. Garabini smoothed the end of his dinosaur tie.

"Uh," Vin paused. "Could you go over number six please?" His sister wasn't the only one who could come up with a quick response.

As Mr. Garabini discussed problem number six, Kam debated his next move. Should he steal the statue back from T.J.? He couldn't have moved it far. It had to be somewhere in the building, probably in T.J.'s own backpack which was in the closet in Mrs. Harris's room. Should he simply show up in the church after school and write an explanation of what happened on his whiteboard for Mr. Wallerby? No, he'd never believe that story, especially from a boy who didn't talk.

For the rest of the afternoon, Kam looked for opportunities to search T.J.'s backpack, but they weren't in Mrs. Harris's room again until last period. And then, with T.J. sitting only two seats behind him, there was no way to go to the closet and look through his bag.

By the end of the day, Kam was running out of hope. As they packed their bags, Vin nudged him.

"What are you going to do about...you know?" Vin inclined his head toward T.J. The classroom was filled with chatter about homework and after-school plans.

Kam pulled out his whiteboard. "Follow him. Get statue. Head to church."

Vin took a sly glance toward T.J. and Marc who stood near the closet. "But how are you going to get him to give it up?"

"Give what up?" Analyn pulled up alongside her brother.

In a low voice, Vin explained about the stolen statue.

"What?" Analyn's face turned red. She pushed her one-sided ponytail behind her shoulder and marched up to T.J. "You give it back," she demanded. A couple kids turned their heads.

"Give what back?" T.J. looked her up and down like she was crazy.

"You know what. The statue you stole from Kameron."

At the word *stole*, more heads turned.

"Hey, crazy, I didn't steal nothing from anyone."

Analyn's eyes darted between T.J. and Marc. "One of you has it. Hand it over right now, or I'm telling Mrs. Harris."

"Tell me what, Miss Cheng?" Mrs. Harris stood behind Analyn. She adjusted the tortoise-shell glasses on the end of her nose. "What is going on here?"

T.J. spoke first. "Analyn's calling me a thief."

"You are a thief," Analyn interjected. "Mrs. Harris, Kam had a statue in his backpack this morning, and it's gone now. T.J. took it when he snuck back in the room during recess."

Mrs. Harris's eyes widened a bit. She turned her attention from Analyn to T.J. "Is this true, Mr. Reynolds?"

"No." T.J. opened his backpack. "You can check my stuff if you want."

Kam held his breath. Did he think Mrs. Harris wouldn't dare to check his bag?

Mrs. Harris took the backpack from T.J. and placed it atop a nearby desk. She pulled out a few books and peered inside. Then she unzipped the outer pockets.

"It doesn't appear he's hiding a statue in here." Mrs. Harris twisted around to face Kam. "How big is this statue you're missing?"

Kam held out his hands to indicate a length of ten inches or so.

Mrs. Harris shook her head. "Definitely not in Mr. Reynolds's backpack."

"Then he gave it to Marc to hide it," Analyn said.

Marc held up his hands. "Hey, don't look at me. I don't have it."

"Then you won't object to me checking your backpack, too." Mrs. Harris handed T.J. his backpack while holding out her other hand for Marc's.

Marc surrendered his, and Mrs. Harris repeated the search process.

Moments later, she shook her head again. "I think, Miss Cheng, you owe these two gentlemen an apology. It appears they do not have the item you accused them of stealing."

"But...but..." Analyn faltered.

"Yes, Miss Cheng," T.J. mocked. "You owe us an apology."

Mrs. Harris gave T.J. one of her famous leveling looks. "No need to get snarky, Mr. Reynolds."

The smug smile on T.J.'s face melted into a sour expression.

Analyn let out a heavy breath. "Sorry, T.J. and Marc. Sorry I accused you of stealing."

The final bell rang.

Mrs. Harris turned to Kam. "Mr. Boyd, I hope you find the statue you lost." Her deep blue eyes pierced his for a moment. "I'm sure it was important to you."

Kam nodded and looked down. What was he to do now? Who else might have stolen the statue? Any hope he had for keeping St. Jude's open was quickly slipping away.

As the students filed out, Analyn called to her brother, "C'mon, Mom's picking us up right away. Sorry about the statue, Kam."

He gave Analyn an understanding nod. He appreciated what she'd done. It took guts to stand up to T.J.

As he made his way to the classroom door, laughter floated out from the hallway. T.J. and Marc had just left the room. Something gnawed at Kam's stomach. He reached for the yo-yo in his pocket. Out in the hallway, T.J. and Marc headed toward the far exit, the one that led toward the church, not the school parking lot on the opposite side. What were they doing going that way? He hesitated in the hallway. Should he follow them? He had to go that way anyway to meet with Mr. Wallerby and explain what happened.

"Bye, Kam," Vin called. He was headed toward the usual exit. "Call me later to tell me how things go with"—he lowered his voice—"the lawyer."

Kam waved to Vin, Analyn, and Nakia as they headed out. Then he moved slowly down the hallway, the kids from the younger grades passing by him on their way to the pick-up exit. Kam felt a bit like an overgrown bass swimming upstream against a tide of guppies. He walked slowly enough for T.J. and Marc to get ahead so he could follow them undetected.

Brightly colored superhero bags and tiny princess backpacks waddled past Kam. The little kids seemed so happy to be going home. Kam wished he could feel the same way, but he had to face the lawyer and let him know he'd lost the treasure.

As he neared the east exit, two muffled voices drifted through the double doors. Kam flattened himself against the wall and listened.

"Good idea to stash it here." Marc's deep voice was easily recognized.

"Only an idiot would have kept it in the classroom."

Kam could hear them thrashing through the bushes.

"C'mon." T.J.'s voice again. "The guy texted that he'd meet me in the church."

The church? Mr. Wallerby!

CHAPTER THIRTY-TWO

Kam waited by the exit for half a minute. The school was emptying out. A couple of fourth graders bounced down the hallway, chatting about their favorite video game. When Kam felt he'd given T.J. and Marc enough time to head into the church, he peered through the narrow window beside the heavy door. T.J. and Marc were no longer in sight.

Kam left the school and looked at the thick bushes along the edge of the building. T.J. must have stashed the statue before heading back out to recess, then texted the lawyer to say he had the treasure.

Taking a deep breath, he headed past the rectory and into the church. Would the lawyer believe he had found the treasure first?

His eyes adjusted slowly to the relative darkness of the church. He had entered through the side entrance the students used for school Masses. A light shone on the tabernacle, and some dull sunrays filtered through the thick, stained-glass windows. Compared to the churches in the city, St. Jude's was relatively plain. The walls were dark wood. The stained-glass windows had pretty designs but were nothing like the intricate pictures at St. Stanislaus. The cobblestone flooring of St. Jude's looked dull after the shiny inlaid floors of St. John Cantius. The walls and ceiling lacked the vibrant colors of Holy Trinity. There were no murals or Latin prayers written on these walls, and the podium was smooth, dark wood, nothing like the intricate carvings on the Ambo of the Evangelists back at Holy Name Cathedral.

And yet, there was still something calming and peaceful about St. Jude's. Something in its simplicity eased the tension that had been building. A simple statue of the Holy Family caught Kam's attention. He'd passed it many times before, but he paused now to look at the infant Jesus, his mother Mary, and Joseph. He thought about his own little family. If his dad were still around, would he be proud of Kam for trying to save St. Jude's, even if he failed in his attempt?

Voices from the front entrance carried through the church. He hurried down the center aisle as the glass doors to the vestibule opened. A tall man in a business suit with a gray goatee and wire-framed glasses stepped inside. He walked to the last pew and genuflected, his gaze on the altar at the opposite end of the church. Behind him sauntered Marc and T.J., who held the tissue-wrapped statue in his right arm as if he were running with a football.

T.J. spotted Kam right away. "What are you doing here, Dork Face?"

The man in the business suit shot T.J. a disgusted face. "We're in a church. You'll keep your tone and your words civil." The man looked toward Kam. "I believe this is the other young man I'm supposed to be meeting here. You are Mr. Kameron Boyd, are you not?"

Kam nodded.

The man extended his hand. "I'm Mr. Wallerby, Edward Engelbert's attorney."

Engelbert? Kam was so shocked he nearly forgot to shake the lawyer's hand. Great Uncle Edward was Edward Engelbert, as in "Old Man Engelbert"? But wait, Old Man Engelbert was still alive, so it couldn't be him. Was it a relative of his? And how was he or T.J. related to him? T.J. always ignored Old Man Engelbert. They certainly didn't act like family.

"Why are you meeting *him?*" T.J. asked. "I texted you that *I* have the treasure."

"Yes, I know," Mr. Wallerby said, "but so did this young man. My guess is one of you only *thinks* he has the right item. Shall we sit?" Mr. Wallerby gestured to the pews. T.J. and Marc sat at the ends of two adjoining pews. Mr. Wallerby and Kam sat across the aisle from them.

"So who wants to go first?"

T.J. smirked. "Why don't we let the loser go first? Go ahead, Kam. Show Mr. Wallerby what you've got."

Kam pulled out his whiteboard and his marker. Out of the corner of his eye, he saw Mr. Wallerby frown. As quickly as he could, Kam scrawled a message.

I had the treasure first, but T.J. stole it.

He held the whiteboard for the lawyer to read.

"Can you prove you had the treasure first?" Mr. Wallerby asked.

Kam shook his head.

"So how am I to believe you?"

He shrugged. St. Jude's slipped further away. T.J. would sell the statue for a fortune and use the money to buy games and probably an expensive car on his sixteenth birthday.

"Did you lose your voice?" Mr. Wallerby asked.

T.J. and Marc both snorted.

"Nah," T.J. said. "He just doesn't talk. Got some kind of problem. You know"—he twirled his finger near his temple—"a mental one."

Kam transferred the marker for his whiteboard to his left hand and reached into his pocket with his right. He wanted to grab his yo-yo and hurl it at T.J.

"Perhaps it would be best if you showed me what you have," Mr. Wallerby said to T.J.

"Yeah, sure, let's make this all official. I've got plans for this money." T.J. snickered as he unwrapped the statue from the tissue paper.

Once again, Kam's heart pounded in his chest. This was it. T.J. was going to win, and he'd be sent back to a school where he had no friends and the teachers didn't understand him. Nakia would end up in a school she didn't like, and the Chengs would end up in boarding school.

T.J. held up the statue of the shepherd boy. "Here ya go," he said. "I don't know what makes it so special. Was it made by Michelangelo or something?"

Mr. Wallerby's forehead creased as he stepped across the aisle. "May I see it?"

T.J. handed it over. "As long as you give me credit for being the finder."

Without any such commitment, Wallerby took the statue gingerly from T.J. and flipped it over to look at the underside of the shepherd's feet. "Well, this definitely wasn't made by Michelangelo, but it is Italian."

All three boys stood up and crowded around the lawyer. Mr. Wallerby was rather tall, but Kam could see what was printed on the bottom of the shepherd's feet: Castelano © 1944.

"See, it's old," T.J. said.

Kam scratched his head. Why hadn't he thought to look at the shepherd's feet before? 1944 was a long time ago, but did that make the statue old enough to be really valuable?

"Is this the treasure you claim to have found first?" Mr. Wallerby asked him.

Kam tried to look Mr. Wallerby in the eye, but he was too nervous. His eyes fell back to the shepherd boy still in the lawyer's hands before he nodded his assent.

Mr. Wallerby sighed. "The good news is that we won't have to worry about which of you found the statue first. The bad news is you're both wrong. This statue isn't the treasure."

CHAPTER THIRTY-THREE

Kam tried to read the lawyer's face. The corner of his mouth was turned up slightly. Was he kidding?

"No way," T.J. stood up. "This statue has to be it. We answered all the riddles. We followed all the clues. This is the treasure."

"I'm sorry, Mr. Reynolds, but this isn't the treasure Edward Engelbert hoped you'd find."

"How could that be? Are there more clues?" T.J. crossed his arms.

"No."

"You must not have told us everything," T.J. insisted.

"I've given you all the instructions your great uncle left. From here on out, you'll simply have to use your smarts."

"What about the statue? It must be worth something."

Kam rolled his eyes. T.J. was always looking for an angle.

"I'm sure it's worth something to whoever is missing it from their Nativity set," Mr. Wallerby said, "but as a collector's piece, I don't think it's worth much at all. Less than a hundred, for sure."

That sounded like a lot of money to Kam, but a hundred dollars was chump change for guys like T.J. and Marc.

"Ah, man, Great Uncle Edward was just messing with us. There's no treasure at all. Come on, Marcs-man, this treasure hunt's for losers."

T.J. and Marc huffed their way out of the church. Mr. Wallerby turned to Kam.

"Did you really find this statue first?"

Kam's heart skipped a beat. Had Mr. Wallerby not told T.J. the truth but simply lied to get rid of him?

He nodded.

"Did you find anything else with it? A note perhaps?"

Kam nodded again and reached for his backpack. He'd slipped the typewritten message into the outer pocket earlier this morning. He pulled it out now and presented it to the lawyer.

Mr. Wallerby unfolded the paper and read the message silently. The corners of his mouth turned up in a little grin.

Kam reached for his whiteboard.

Is it the treasure?

"The note?" Mr. Wallerby raised an eyebrow.

Kam nodded.

The lawyer's face broke out into a big grin. "No, I'm afraid not, but I'm sure Father Fitzgerald would appreciate getting his shepherd boy back. My guess is the St.

Jude nativity set has been missing this important character for several decades." He returned the statue to Kam.

The shepherd boy looked so plain in his hands now. Only a few hours ago, he thought it was the answer to all his problems. Now, he was simply a piece of a Nativity scene that would finally be returned home.

Kam walked up the long center aisle and placed the statue on the altar. Father Fitzgerald would find it there, and Kam wouldn't have to give any explanations. Before turning back around, he looked up at the large crucifix hanging above the priest's chair. Maybe God didn't want St. Jude's to stay open. Maybe He had other plans for Kam.

With a sigh, he turned around to walk out. He was surprised to see Mr. Wallerby still standing at the end of the pews.

When Kam reached him, Mr. Wallerby said, "You seem like a nice young man, Kameron Boyd, so I'm going to tell you a little secret."

Kam stared at Mr. Wallerby's right hand, which clasped the leather handle of his briefcase. He didn't know if he wanted to hear a secret. No good had come of all the hard work, riddles, and secrets of the last few days.

"My client wanted his heir to be the kind of young person who would make him proud, so I think he'd be okay with me giving you this one teensy little hint. The treasure that you're looking for...well, it's a lot closer than you think."

And with that, Mr. Wallerby looked to the altar, genuflected, and strode out of the church.

CHAPTER THIRTY-FOUR

Kam stood motionless. What had Mr. Wallerby just told him? The game was still on. The treasure was still out there. And it wasn't far away!

He spun in a circle. Did that mean the treasure was somewhere in the church? He searched under the pews. No, that was ridiculous. The treasure wouldn't be in plain sight.

After fishing his phone out of his pocket, Kam scrolled to the final clue.

> To find the treasure, you must seek it deep within the church. You might say it lies within the body of Christ.

Deep within the church? The basement? No, St. Jude's Church didn't have a basement. The body of Christ? The only statue of Christ St. Jude's had was the one hanging on the crucifix. It couldn't be there.

Kam pounded the palm of his right hand against his forehead. How could the answer be so close yet so far away?

If only he knew more about this Edward Engelbert.
Maybe then he'd have an idea of how his brain worked,
and then he could figure out what this last clue really
meant.

There was only one option left. He had to talk to
someone who knew Edward Engelbert.

Kam sent a text to the Mystery Riddler.

You're…

He paused a moment with his typing. There was no
way around this.

You're the one we call "Old Man Engelbert," aren't
u? I think we need to talk.

Kam took a deep breath before hitting the send button. What did he have to lose? He sent off the text and
headed toward the bike rack outside school. He had his
response by the time he'd unlocked his bike.

Yes, I am. And you're right. We must talk. Your
house. Tomorrow night. 7 P.M.

Vin and Analyn couldn't believe his story. Vin had put
Kam on speaker phone so they both could hear what had
happened.

Analyn shared the story with Nakia later that night,
so that by the time they gathered at their corner of the
lot during recess the next day, they all knew Kam would
have to face Old Man Engelbert that night.

"I can't believe he was the Master Riddler," Analyn
said.

"I know," Kam muttered.

"Are you related to him?" Nakia swatted at a fly that buzzed past.

"I don't think so."

"Will you be able to talk to him?" Nakia asked. If the question had come from anyone else, Kam might have thought it rude. But this was Nakia. He knew she wasn't making fun of him.

"I've never had trouble talking inside my house before. It's only outside my house when there are adults around."

Nakia smiled at him. "I'm sure you'll do fine, Kam. Learn as much as you can about Edward Engelbert. You can't let any of the other heirs figure it out first."

———

Despite his friends' reassurances, Kam grew more anxious as the afternoon ticked by. At home, he tried to think of a way to bring up Old Man Engelbert's arrival. He should tell Gram and his mother, but he didn't know how to start the conversation. *Oh by the way, I came* this *close to solving all the riddles and winning the fortune, and Old Man Engelbert is coming over to help.*

As he cleared the dinner table, Kam stole a glance through the kitchen window. The days were slowly getting longer, but at the moment, the sun was fading fast. The blue sky was already darkening, and the horizon was streaked with shades of gold and pink. Kam looked at the clock on the oven. It was almost seven.

"I have someone coming over tonight," Kam blurted out.

"Really?" Gram didn't sound surprised.

Kam looked at her in time to see her exchange a look with his mother. Was that a smirk on his mother's face?

"Your grandmother's expecting a visitor, too," his mom said.

"Yes, I've asked Serafina Harris to join us this evening."

"Mrs. Harris?" Kam croaked.

Gram picked up a sponge and wiped down the stove. "I thought you liked Mrs. Harris."

"I do," Kam said. His mind whirled. Mrs. Harris here tonight? With Old Man Engelbert coming? It was bad enough his mom and Gram would learn he'd gone into the city without permission, but now Mrs. Harris would know, too. What kind of awful punishment would the three of them cook up?

The front doorbell rang so suddenly Kam nearly dropped the glasses he was carrying.

"I'll get it." He set the glasses into the dishwasher and sprinted for the front door.

"If it's Mrs. Harris, send her back here to the kitchen."

As he reached for the doorknob, Kam held his breath. If it was Mrs. Harris, maybe he could whisk her to the kitchen and then keep Old Man Engelbert in the front parlor. Then again, if it was Old Man Engelbert, maybe he could finish up with him before Mrs. Harris even arrived.

Kam swung the door open. On the other side were both Mrs. Harris and Old Man Engelbert.

CHAPTER THIRTY-FIVE

Mrs. Harris wore her trademark purple scarf and tortoise-shell glasses while her right arm held a large tapestry bag. Old Man Engelbert sat in his motorized chair. He wore a jacket that zipped to his neck. Kam thought again of the hole he'd seen in Old Man Engelbert's throat the day he'd pulled his chair out of the mud.

"Good evening, Kameron." Mrs. Harris gave him a small smile.

"Hi, Mrs. Harris." He looked at Old Man Engelbert and willed himself not to use his nickname. "Hi, Mr. Engelbert."

Old Man Engelbert looked up at Mrs. Harris. "You were right," he wheezed. "He does talk."

"In the right situations." Mrs. Harris winked at Kam. "May we come in?"

Stepping aside, Kam made room for both of them to enter. What was he going to do now?

"My grandmother said you could go right back to the kitchen, Mrs. Harris." Maybe he still had a shot at talking to Old Man Engelbert alone.

"I've changed my mind." Gram appeared in the hallway. "Good evening, Serafina."

"Hello, Jackie."

"Charles." Gram nodded to Old Man Engelbert.

"Always a pleasure to see you, Jackie." Old Man Engelbert shifted in his chair.

"Why don't we all settle into the parlor?" Gram gestured with her left hand. In her right, she held one of the tote bags she took to her Zumba classes. "Rebecca," Gram called to Kam's mom in the kitchen, "could you bring some tea please?"

Kam's mom ran into the front hallway, wiping her hands on a towel. "I want to hear what's going on, too."

Kam's heart sunk. Somehow, they all knew something was going on.

Gram grimaced at her daughter-in-law. "Put the kettle on, dear. I'm sure you won't miss any of the good stuff." She turned back to her guests. "Shall we?"

By the time Old Man Engelbert wheeled himself into position in the parlor and Gram and Mrs. Harris took their positions on the sofa, Kam's mom returned from the kitchen. She sat in one of Gram's old wingback chairs, while Kam sat on the edge of the piano bench.

"So, Kameron," Old Man Engelbert began. "Tell me what you learned from the lawyer."

"Um." Words failed him. He looked to his mom who leaned forward, hands clasped on her knees. She was staring straight at him. She would be so disappointed when she found out what he'd done.

He turned to Mrs. Harris, who looked even taller than usual seated next to his petite grandmother. Everyone looked expectantly at him.

"Well..." How could he possibly begin?

"Go ahead, Kam," his mother said. "We know all about your trip into the city."

"You do?" He looked from face to face for confirmation. How could they possibly know? And why hadn't they said something sooner?

Gram turned to Mrs. Harris. "I suppose it's time we let Kam in on our little secret."

"I suppose so." Mrs. Harris reached into her tapestry bag while Gram rifled through her workout bag. Moments later, they pulled on fake glasses and flat caps. Mrs. Harris even pulled out a fake mustache. Only the beige trench coats were missing.

"You!" Kam nearly slid off the piano bench. "You two are the old geezers who followed us?"

Mrs. Harris let out a laugh that was half snort. Gram's laugh was more of a chortle.

"You didn't think we'd let you roam around the city alone, did you?" Gram asked.

"But how did you even know I was going to the city?"

Mrs. Harris took off the fake glasses and returned her usual tortoise-shell ones to her face. "Charles, I think you better start at the beginning."

Old Man Engelbert coughed, a nasty hacking cough that rattled the old man's bones. When he finished, he spoke in his usual mechanical voice. "I'm the younger brother of Edward Engelbert, who passed away recently. My brother was a bit of a trickster as a child, often playing pranks on me and our younger sister Ann. Most of his jokes were harmless, but sometimes, his actions had unexpected consequences. For example, you may have noticed that the gym at St. Jude's is newer than the rest of the building. When we were students there, my brother set off fireworks during recess. Some of the burning embers landed on the gym roof, and before long, a sizeable portion had been destroyed."

Kam hadn't really noticed the difference between the two parts of the school. It all seemed old to him.

"At the time this happened, our father was a very rich man. He paid for the repairs, and Edward never learned his lesson. Only when he lost his son Michael in a house fire did he began to realize how dangerous his actions could be."

Old Man Engelbert took in a deep breath, his throat rattling. He rested a hand on his heart.

"You must stop blaming yourself, Charles," Mrs. Harris said. "That cigarette could have been anyone's—Edward's, his wife's, even Michael's. Far too many of us smoked in those days."

"Thank you, Serafina. Lord knows I've paid the price for my smoking." He gestured toward his throat.

The words came out before Kam could stop them. "So you do have a...?"

"A hole in my throat?" Old Man Engelbert unzipped the top of his jacket. A strange knob was attached where the hole had been. "The day you saved me from the mud, I didn't have my hands-free device with me. Yes, the hole is from cancer caused by years of smoking, but we're getting off topic."

Kam breathed a sigh of relief. He didn't want to know more about cancers that caused holes in your throat.

"Toward the end of his life, my brother regretted his earlier hijinks. I think he thought his will would be a way to make up for it. He decided to leave his fortune to one heir, but that person had to be someone who understood the true value of things. He thought the riddles he left behind would determine the worthiest heir."

"So how did I end up one of the possible heirs?" Kam shifted his weight on the piano bench.

"Edward's will stipulated that his heir had to be a child—younger than seventeen—and either a current St. Jude's student or a recent alum."

"Edward Engelbert was T.J. Reynolds's great uncle, right?" Kam asked.

"Yes, and as a current St. Jude's student, he qualified. His cousins, Amanda and Jeffrey, also qualified since they graduated within the last few years."

"You've met T.J.'s cousin Amanda," Mrs. Harris said.

An image of three blonde teenagers with huge sunglasses flashed before his eyes. "Oh! The blonde girl."

Mrs. Harris nodded. "And you saw Jeffrey, but probably had no idea he was playing the game. He was one of the teenage boys who boarded the train the same time you did."

"And we did—barely," Gram added.

"Oh, yeah," Kam said. "What happened to them?"

Mrs. Harris sniffed. "Ran into some pretty girls downtown and got sidetracked."

"Jeffrey is a lot like his great uncle Charles," Gram said, looking pointedly at Old Man Engelbert.

He gave a wheezy chuckle. "I'm afraid you're correct."

"But that still doesn't explain how I'm involved," Kam said.

"As my brother Edward was dying, he realized that the kind of heir he'd hoped for might not exist within his own family. His only son Michael had died, and our sister Ann's grandchildren—T.J., Amanda, and Jeffrey—reminded Edward too much of himself as a child. Frivolous. Spoiled. Self-centered. He also knew that my dear departed wife and I had no children of our own. So he allowed for a 'mystery cousin,' a chance for me to pick a potential heir—sort of an adopted grandson. His only request was that I pick someone who valued St. Jude's, someone who would make him proud to be his heir."

Kam pushed himself further back on the piano bench to steady himself. "So you could have picked any kid at St. Jude's? You could have picked Analyn or Vin or Nakia."

Old Man Engelbert nodded. "I went to my old friends for advice."

"Watch who you're calling old," Gram snapped.

Mrs. Harris held up a hand like she was silencing her classroom. "You see, Kam, your grandmother, Mr. Engelbert, Sister Maria Ann, and I all attended St. Jude's together. When it was time for him to pick a potential heir to represent his branch of the family, he came to me for advice. He asked which of my students he thought most embodied the spirit of St. Jude School and who would miss St. Jude's the most if it closed. I, of course, thought of you."

CHAPTER THIRTY-SIX

Kam let the news sink in. Mrs. Harris had recommended him. Of all the students at St. Jude—granted, the school was small, but still—his teacher had picked him to be the potential heir to a fortune.

"So Mrs. Harris is the reason you sent me the riddles," Kam said.

"She recommended you, but I had to make sure for myself. That's why I drove my chair into the mud last Wednesday."

"You did that on purpose?" Kam stood up.

"I had to know what you were made of. My brother's fortune is worth millions. I didn't want it getting into the wrong hands. I knew you were the right man for the job when you got off your bike and rescued me from the mud. Tried to get you to say your name to make sure I had the right boy, but of course, that didn't work." Old Man Engelbert started to laugh, but it led to another coughing fit. When his coughing died down, he said, "Then I had to ask your mom and Gram for permission."

"I almost didn't give it." His mother pushed back her dirty-blonde hair. "I thought it'd be way too dangerous. I told your grandmother I hadn't let you roam Milwaukee alone when we lived in Wisconsin. I wasn't going to let you roam Chicago alone."

"And I assured your mother that Serafina and I would be following you the whole way. Besides, a boy needs to step outside his comfort zone every now and then."

Mrs. Harris looked at Kam. "We never would have let you come in harm's way."

"So now it's your turn, young man," Old Man Engelbert said. "Tell us what Mr. Wallerby had to say."

Kam took a deep breath and then let it out. "The statue of the shepherd boy was not the treasure. It belongs to St. Jude's, but he said it wasn't the right thing. He said the treasure isn't far away, but I have no idea what it is."

"Shepherd boy." Mrs. Harris gasped. "Why, of course."

Kam looked around at the adults. Only his mother looked as confused as he felt.

Old Man Engelbert answered the unspoken question. "While we were students at St. Jude, the shepherd boy went missing from the church Nativity set. Rumors of it being stolen spread, but it was never recovered. My guess is that the missing statue was another of my brother's pranks, one he regretted later but didn't know how to rectify, so he let his heir do it for him."

"So is that it?" Kam asked. "We've run out of riddles, the game is up? No one gets the fortune?"

Old Man Engelbert shook his head. "No, if Mr. Wallerby told you the answer is closer than you think, then the treasure's still out there, and there's still a way to find it." He reached into a pocket along the side of his chair and pulled out two pieces of paper. "Here are all the riddles. Each of the other potential heirs received a copy of them. I decided to text them to you one at a time. My guess is my brother had a reason for putting them in this order."

"What do you mean?" Kam took the papers from Engelbert.

"My brother loved codes and ciphering. He was very methodical. I know some of the riddles led to the same churches, but those riddles weren't right next to each other. He must have had a reason for this." Engelbert shrugged. "Maybe that will help you find the answer you're seeking."

"So you think there's still a chance I might become the heir?"

"All you have to do is beat T.J., Amanda, and Jeffrey to it."

Kam scanned the list of riddles. A second page had been stapled to the back. This one was a printout of an email from Mr. Wallerby to Engelbert. It included the final instruction about seeking the treasure deep within the church.

"And if I don't find the treasure before the school meeting tomorrow night," Kam asked, "what happens to St. Jude's?"

Mrs. Harris sighed. "I'm afraid there's not much you can do about the school, Kam. The parish has been slowly shrinking over the last few decades. There aren't enough students to keep the place open."

"But if the money problems were solved…Mr. Engelbert, your family's rich, you must have a lot of money."

"I wish I did. I'm afraid my story is a bit like the prodigal son. Our father gave Edward, Ann, and me our shares of the inheritance when we reached eighteen. I spent mine foolishly. Ann was a penny pincher who married well, and Charles was a savvy investor. Trust me, if I had the money to save our little school, I'd gladly donate it."

In the kitchen, the tea kettle whistled its steamy protest at the boiling water inside. Kam's mom excused herself to prepare the tea while the other adults chatted about the closing of the school. Kam refused to listen. He retreated within himself, thinking about the riddles and how he might possibly solve them the way Edward Engelbert had intended.

CHAPTER THIRTY-SEVEN

The sun had set, the tea had all been drunk, and Kam's mom had flipped on the antique lamps in the parlor. Looking at his watch, Kam figured the adults would be leaving soon, but as his mother cleared away the teacups, Old Man Engelbert turned his attention to Kam.

"There's still one thing I don't understand." His voice was as robotic as ever, but his blue eyes were bright and piercing. "Why is it you can talk here in your house with me and your teacher, but if you met us at school or at church, you couldn't?"

Kam lifted his shoulders. "I just can't."

"Has it always been like this?"

"Oh no." His mother returned from the kitchen. "He was quite the talker in kindergarten. Learned to read at an early age. His teacher even had him help the other kids who struggled."

"So what happened?" Old Man Engelbert asked.

Kam squirmed on the piano bench. "First grade was different."

"Well, something must have happened between kindergarten and first grade," Engelbert insisted.

"His father passed away." Gram's curt reply was nearly enough to end the conversation, but Kam's mother kept it going.

"I'm sure that had nothing to do with it. Jerry's death was months before Kam started first grade. He was fine all that summer."

Mrs. Harris reached into her pocket and fingered her rosary beads. "His father's death was rather sudden, wasn't it?"

His mom nodded. "It was a car accident. He was on his way to Kam's kindergarten graduation."

Kam shut his eyes at the memory. He didn't want to picture it all over again, but the memory was so vivid. He stood on the platform with all the other kindergarteners in their plastic graduation caps. Then his mother suddenly stood up in the middle of the sea of parents, her cell phone in hand. She rushed to the stage, pulled Kam off, and yanked him out right in the middle of the ceremony, breathlessly muttering to the teachers about a family emergency and needing to get to the hospital right away.

Despite the roughness of Old Man Engelbert's voice, his next words were gentle. "You were very close with your father, weren't you?"

Kam kept his eyes closed as his mother responded for him. "Oh yes, Jerry was a very devoted father. He's the one who got Kam interested in yo-yoing."

"He's the national junior champion," Gram boasted. Kam opened his eyes to see his grandmother step across the room to where his trophies were displayed on the mantel. "See? Look at all these awards."

"What kind of yo-yo do you use?" Engelbert asked.

"He has all sorts of yo-yos."

Kam hated it when his mother spoke for him, especially at home when he was capable of speaking for himself.

"Show Mr. Engelbert that 1970s Duncan of your father's."

He cringed. "I can't, Mom."

"Of course, you can. You always have it in your pocket."

Kam pulled the newer yo-yo out of his pocket.

"Where's your father's yo-yo?" Gram asked.

"Upstairs." Kam could barely get the next few words out. "It's broken."

"Broken?" his mother exclaimed. "That's not possible. You always take such good care of it."

Mrs. Harris leaned forward. "Kameron, what happened?"

"Some guys got a hold of it and...it just fell and broke, okay?" No need to mention who broke it. Tattling on T.J. and Marc would only result in more bullying.

"Who? What guys?" Gram demanded.

Mrs. Harris rested a hand on her friend's arm. "I can make a pretty good guess."

Kam locked eyes with Mrs. Harris for a moment. *Please don't make me tell.*

"They should be held responsible," Gram insisted. "They should buy him a new one. It was a collector's item."

Mrs. Harris kept her eyes on Kam. "Let Kameron and me take care of it."

"I should get going," Old Man Engelbert said. "Sometime, young man, you'll have to show me your yo-yo tricks. Tonight, though, it's way past this old man's bedtime." He gave a little chortle.

After saying good-bye, Kam headed up to his room. He had less than twenty-four hours before the school meeting at which the fate of St. Jude's would be decided, and he still had no idea how to solve the final riddle.

CHAPTER THIRTY-EIGHT

Despite a brainstorming session at recess the next day, Kam and his friends still had no further ideas. All the talk at school was that no one had come up with a plan to solve the school's financial problems. That night, Sister Maria Ann and Mr. DeLuca would announce the closing of the school.

To make things worse, they were supposed to have picked out their famous person for their oral report, and Kam had to admit to Mrs. Harris that he still didn't have a topic. She looked disappointed, but didn't press too hard, simply told him he'd better concentrate on finding one soon, as the presentations would be next week.

By the time he got home, Kam wanted to bury his head under a mountain of pillows. He had failed to become the heir to Edward Engelbert's fortune. He had failed to save St. Jude's. He couldn't even pick a person for his report.

Rifling through the papers on his desk, Kam found the copy of the riddles Old Man Engelbert had given him last night. He still had a few hours until the meeting. He might as well give it one last shot.

Old Man Engelbert said his brother had been very methodical. He put the clues in a particular order for a reason. Kam took out a blank piece of paper and jotted down the answers to the clues.

Us (Nobis)

Ox

Matrimony (Wedding)

Hammer

Evangelists

Red

Egypt

Tapping his pencil against the edge of his desk, Kam looked for any sort of pattern in the words. There were all nouns—or pronouns. They were all single-word answers. They didn't make a sentence if you read them straight down.

Maybe it had something more to do with the order of the churches. Kam went downstairs to the den, turned on the computer, and opened up Google maps. He pinpointed each church they visited, and then drew lines connecting them all. Perhaps they would make a shape that represented what the treasure was.

But when he was done connecting all the dots, he had a weird triangle with a funny arm on top.

Kam turned the paper around in multiple directions, but he couldn't make any sense out of the strange design.

He went back to his room and decided to have a go at the words again. Maybe the answers made an acronym. He read down the first letter of each word: Uomhere. No, that wasn't anything.

He paused with his pencil hovering over the page. What if he used the Latin word *nobis* instead of the English word *us* and used *wedding* instead of *matrimony*? He scribbled out the first letters again. Now the beginning of each answer spelled *Nowhere*.

Kam threw down his pencil. "Nowhere," he muttered aloud. "That's exactly where I'm going with these clues. Absolutely nowhere."

Maybe it was all a cruel joke. Great Uncle Edward was known for being a prankster. Maybe he'd decided to play one last final gag on his descendants—both genetic and hand-picked.

"Kameron, it's time for dinner," Gram called.

With a heavy heart, Kam trudged downstairs. After saying grace, the meal was eaten in relative silence. Gram had found a substitute instructor to teach her Zumba class so she could attend the meeting with Kam and his mom.

"You don't have to go with us to the meeting tonight if you don't want to," his mother said.

"I know." Kam pushed a few remaining peas around on his plate. "I want to go."

When he could force no more food down his throat, Kam cleared his place and excused himself. He had only twenty minutes before they left for the meeting.

At his desk upstairs, Kam picked up the list of riddles. He flipped over the first page to read the printed email from Wallerby to Engelbert with the final clue.

Kam squinted at the page. This final riddle wasn't written exactly the same way Engelbert had sent it. A few words were capitalized that Engelbert had texted lower-case—Church and Body—so that the final clue really read: *To find the treasure, you must seek it deep within the Church. You might say it lies within the Body of Christ.*

What had Mrs. Harris said about those words being capitalized? When church was written with a lowercase 'c,' it meant the building. When it was written with a capital 'C,' it meant the people who make up "the Church." When *Body of Christ* is capitalized, it doesn't mean his corpse, it means us, the people.

Kam sat up straight in his chair. He knew where the treasure was.

CHAPTER THIRTY-NINE

The first thing Kam did was text Mr. Wallerby to ask him to come to the meeting at St. Jude's. He didn't know how far away the lawyer was, but he hoped he could get to the school in time. Then he texted Vin. At recess, Analyn, Vin, and Nakia had said they weren't coming. They didn't want to hear about St. Jude's closing, but Kam really needed Vin to be there—more importantly, he needed Vin's laptop.

After sending off his texts, Kam darted downstairs as his mother and grandmother were coming up.

"We'll be leaving in a few minutes," Gram said.

"Okay." Kam didn't stop to turn around. "I'll be in the den."

Pulling his yo-yo out of his pocket, Kam gave it a little squeeze while the computer warmed up. Then he set the yo-yo next to the monitor, flipped on the web cam, and began recording. He had only a few minutes to put his plan into action. There would be no time for second takes on this video. He had to get out what he wanted to say as quickly and clearly as he could. This was his only way to have his voice heard, and he said a silent prayer of thanks that Mrs. Harris had given him the idea of videotaping his oral report.

The mouse hovered over the record button. Could he do this? Would his tongue freeze up? What if he chickened out? No. He had to do this. Mrs. Harris said there were some things in life worth stepping outside of your comfort zone for. This was one of them.

Minutes later, Kam downloaded the video onto a flash drive. Vin texted that he'd bring his laptop to the meeting, but he wanted to know why.

Kam texted a short reply.

To save our school!

Before he knew it, he was in the backseat of Gram's car, his flash drive in his left pocket. Kam reached inside the other pocket for his yo-yo.

Empty! He had left the yo-yo in the den next to the computer. Kam tried not to panic, but without his yo-yo to comfort him, his right hand tugged at his pant leg.

The school gym was packed. More people had shown up tonight than at last week's meeting. Were people expecting a train wreck and had come to watch the spectacle?

His family took a seat in the third row while parents and a few of the older school children talked in groups. Some people were already seated, but others stood sharing whatever rumors they'd heard.

A couple minutes later, Vin, Analyn, and their mother took seats in the row behind Kam.

Vin lifted the laptop over the folding chairs. "Here you go. What have you got in mind?"

Kam looked around at the many adults in the gym. There was no way for him to tell Vin his plan aloud, so he simply held up his flash drive and waved it at his best friend.

"Unless you've got a million dollars stored on that flash drive, I don't think that's gonna save our school."

Next to Vin, Analyn tugged at her one-sided ponytail. "I hope you know what you're doing, Kam."

Kam pointed to himself and then held up two fingers as if to say, "Me, too."

A motorized chair whirred its way up the aisle. Old Man Engelbert stopped at the end of Kam's row.

"Just wanted to stop by and see my adopted grand-son," Engelbert wheezed.

Kam gave him a small smile. He was dying to tell him what he'd found, but Engelbert would find out at the same time everyone else did.

"Don't worry about not finding the treasure, son. I'm proud of you anyway. Father Fitzgerald told me he found the shepherd boy on the altar. Says next Christmas will be the first time St. Jude's has had a complete Nativity set in over sixty years." Old Man Engelbert reached into the side pocket of his chair. "Brought something for ya. I know it won't replace your father's, but I thought you might like it nonetheless." Old Man Engelbert held out a shiny orange Duncan whistler. Kam recognized it instantly. Duncan hadn't made these since the 1950s. Due to holes drilled on the sides, the yo-yo actually whistled as it spun.

"Go ahead. Take it," Old Man Engelbert said.

Gingerly, Kam reached for it.

"That's very nice of you, Mr. Engelbert," Kam's mother said.

"It's a little older than your father's, I'm sure. Had this back in 1948."

Kam's eyes widened.

"Didn't know I used to do a little yo-yoing myself, did ya?" Engelbert's eyes gleamed.

Kam shook his head.

"Keep a good eye on it now," Old Man Engelbert said, and he wheeled away.

"Now wasn't that nice of Mr. Engelbert?" his mom asked.

Gram snorted. "Just trying to make up for his past sins before he goes the way of his brother."

On the stage, Sister Maria Ann tapped on the microphone. "Could we have everyone take a seat? We'd like to start tonight's meeting."

People shuffled into the folding chairs. Father Fitzgerald and Mr. DeLuca stood on either side of Sister Maria Ann. All three of them looked grim. Part of Kam hoped they'd found a way to solve the financial crisis on their own. Maybe he wouldn't even need to show the video he'd made. But the look on their faces didn't give him much hope.

When people had taken their seats, Sister Maria Ann resumed talking. "As you know, the enrollment at St. Jude's has been declining rather steadily the last ten years. Without raising tuition drastically, the school simply can't keep itself funded. The parish financial committee has looked at ways the parish might be able to help out, but as Mr. DeLuca pointed out last week, the Archdiocese does not allow a parish to fund the majority of a school's bills. The school must be able to support itself, with only limited assistance from the parish budget."

Sister Maria Ann looked to Father Fitzgerald, who nodded at her. "Therefore, it is with a heavy heart, that I must announce the closing of St. Jude School."

Murmuring erupted among the audience members. Kam could hear people saying, "I knew it," but he ignored them. He picked up Vin's laptop and exited the third row.

"Kameron," his mother called. "Where are you going?"

Sister Maria Ann banged a small gavel on the podium to get people's attention. Kam stepped right up on the stage and walked toward her. Sister Maria Ann did a double take.

"Young man, what are you doing up here?"

Kam lifted the laptop as if that alone would explain his strange behavior.

"What are you doing?" the principal insisted.

He set the laptop down on top of the podium and pulled the flash drive from his pocket.

"Kameron, you must sit down."

He shook his head and began searching for the cable that would project his video from the laptop onto the screen at the back of the stage.

The crowd had started to quiet, and Kam now heard snickering among the adults as he fumbled around the stage, picking up cables.

Mrs. Harris stood up from her front row seat and stepped onto the stage. "Kameron, what are you doing?"

Kam looked at the worried expression on his favorite teacher's face. He pointed to the flash drive in his hand and then to the laptop and then to the screen.

"You've got something to show us?"

Kam nodded, picking up the correct cable and connecting it to Vin's laptop.

"Did you"—Mrs. Harris covered the microphone on the podium—"did you find it?"

Stopping a moment while pushing the flash drive into the laptop, Kam smiled at Mrs. Harris.

She smiled back. "Sister Maria Ann, I think young Mr. Boyd has something he needs to show us. Something that might make you very happy."

"Serafina," Sister whispered harshly, "this isn't the time to indulge students in their antics just so they can amuse themselves."

"Oh, I think you'll be the one to get a kick out of this." Mrs. Harris stepped up to the microphone. "Ladies and gentlemen, one of our finest young minds here at St. Jude's would like to share a little something with you." Her eyes darted through the audience until her gaze settled on the back row. T.J. sat beside his father, and both of them had their arms crossed. "T.J. Reynolds," Mrs. Harris's voiced boomed through the microphone, "would you please shut off the lights for us?"

Both T.J. and his father started.

"I'm sorry," Mrs. Harris said. "I'll be more specific. Theodore Jefferson Reynolds, the *fourth*, please turn off the lights."

T.J. looked around like she still might be talking to someone else, but Mrs. Harris kept her eyes right on him. Reluctantly, he got up and shut off the lights, but not before Kam caught a glimpse of Mr. Wallerby in his usual dark suit and tie walking in through the gym door. Kam gave him a wave, and Mr. Wallerby nodded in recognition.

The room went dark as the video was projected on the screen behind Kam. This was it. If he were right, everything would be fine. If he were wrong, he'd be humiliated. He would have put himself out there in front of everyone—his friends, his mom, Gram, Old Man Engelbert, his principal, his pastor, tons of parents, T.J., everyone—and he'd look like an idiot.

Taking a deep breath, Kam hit play.

CHAPTER FORTY

On the big screen behind him, a giant version of Kam sprung to life. He was seated at the desk in his family's den. His auburn curls nearly fell in his eyes as he bit his lip before beginning.

"Hi, everyone. I'm Kam Boyd. I'm a seventh grader at St. Jude. Some of you may know that I've been named a potential heir to Edward Engelbert and that I've been given a set of riddles to solve. The first to solve the riddles and find Edward Engelbert's hidden treasure becomes the heir to his fortune."

The on-screen Kam took a deep breath, and the off-screen one mimicked his actions.

"I've been working really hard to solve the riddles because I want to give the money to St. Jude's so the school can stay open, but the riddles have been very hard. With the help of my friends, Vin, Analyn, and Nakia, we solved the first seven riddles, but the last clue was super tough. We thought we'd found the treasure when the last clue led us to a statue of a shepherd boy that had been stolen from St. Jude's a long time ago."

Father Fitzgerald caught Kam's eyes from across the stage. Father smiled at him, and Kam felt his cheeks grow warm.

"But when Mr. Wallerby—he's the lawyer taking care of Edward Engelbert's will—saw the statue, he said it wasn't the treasure. So I thought I'd failed. But then I decided to try the riddles again. Maybe Edward Engelbert had left a coded message in there. That's when I figured out that the answers to the seven riddles were an acronym for the word *nowhere*. For the second time, I thought I'd failed. Oh, by the way, Mrs. Harris, thanks for teaching us what acronyms are."

The crowd laughed, and Kam wanted to tuck his head into his body like a turtle.

"Then I looked at the last clue, the one that said we were supposed to look deep within the Church because the answer would be with the Body of Christ. Look." On-screen Kam held up the email with the final clue so that it was right in front of the web cam. "See how Church and Body of Christ are capitalized? That's us. We're the Church. We're the Body of Christ." On-screen Kam pulled the sheet of paper from the camera. "So I finally got it. I know what Edward Engelbert wanted us to find. The treasure is—"

On-screen Kam took in a deep breath. Off-screen Kam held his.

"Us. We're the treasure. You see, it all fits. The shepherd boy. He represents, you know, like the average guy following Jesus. He's not one of the fancy kings. He's not the mother or the father. He's just an average working boy, sort of like us kids here at St. Jude's. And then there's the word *nowhere*. That fits, too, because I didn't need to go anywhere to find the treasure. Kind of like Dorothy and her ruby slippers. I had the answer I needed with me all the time. And the whole Church and Body of Christ, like I said, that's us. We're the treasure because we're the future of the Church. Edward Engelbert insisted that his heir be under the age of 17 and someone who went to St. Jude's because he wanted us to realize that we are the future of the Church. Without us, it doesn't go on."

On-screen Kam scratched his head. "I hope this doesn't make me sound really snobby. I'm not trying to say I'm great or anything. I mean, we're all important. If I'm right, Edward Engelbert wanted us to learn that people are more important than things. The churches we visited last Saturday are really cool and everything, but they're not more important than the people in them."

On-screen Kam paused for a moment. Off-screen Kam was too frightened to look at anyone.

"So I asked Mr. Wallerby if he'd come here tonight because I'm hoping I'm right. I'm hoping I found the treasure Edward Engelbert wanted me to find because if I did, if this makes me the heir to his fortune, I'd like to donate it all to St. Jude's, because this is my school. No, it's more than that. It's part of my family. What's important here at St. Jude's isn't the technology or the clubs or any of the "stuff." It's the people. People like Mrs. Harris who cares about each of us like we were her own grandkids. And Mr. Garabini and Ms. Lawton who try real hard to get us to learn. And Sister Maria Ann who doesn't let us get away with anything."

A few in the crowd snickered. A couple generations of St. Jude students knew not to cross the principal.

"And all my friends at St. Jude's, especially the ones who helped me solve the riddles even though they weren't going to win the prize themselves. They're what's most important. So I want to keep this school open. I want to graduate from here next year. And I want lots of other kids, who maybe don't fit in at other bigger schools, to have a chance to graduate from here, too. So, Mr. Wallerby, I hope you make it to St. Jude's tonight, and I hope I'm right."

On-screen Kam paused again and bit his lip.

"I guess that's all I have to say. Thanks for listening."

On-screen Kam leaned forward and turned off the web cam.

Off-screen Kam closed his eyes momentarily. A choking sound from his right made him open them again. Standing on the other side of the stage, Sister Maria Ann held a hand over her mouth. She took in another quick breath and then sniffled as a tear rolled down her cheek.

Oh no, I've made a nun cry.

The crowd was dead silent.

Mrs. Harris put an arm around Sister Maria Ann. Mr. DeLuca stepped up beside Kam and rested a hand on his shoulder.

The sound of dress shoes clicking their way across the gym floor made everyone turn around. Mr. Wallerby was walking up the center aisle.

Voices in the audience whispered as he stepped onto the stage. With a nod to Kam, the lawyer approached the microphone. He shut Vin's laptop so that the screen behind him went dark.

"T.J. Reynolds," Mr. Wallerby's voice boomed. He hardly needed the microphone. "Would you mind turning the lights back on, please?"

A chair squeaked in the back. Moments later, the lights flickered on.

Mr. Wallerby cleared his throat. "For those of you who haven't guessed yet, I'm Richard Wallerby, the lawyer for Edward Engelbert's estate."

More murmuring from the crowd.

Mr. Wallerby turned to Kam. "You are a very brave, honorable, and intelligent young man, Kameron Boyd. And this so-called treasure you've found..."

Mr. Wallerby paused. Kam was beginning to think he had as much a flair for dramatics as his friend Analyn had.

"Well," Mr. Wallerby continued after the crowd had hushed, "this treasure you've found is absolutely...correct."

Kam felt his knees give out below him. Luckily, Mr. DeLuca was there to catch him.

"If my client were still alive, I'm sure he'd be very happy to claim you as his heir, but as he is no longer with us, I will have the distinct pleasure of naming you heir to the Engelbert fortune."

Kam looked to his mother. Tears streamed down her cheeks faster than she could wipe them with a tissue.

Gram simply beamed, her wrinkles crinkling around her mouth and eyes.

"And Sister Maria Ann." Mr. Wallerby turned his attention in the opposite direction. "You'll be interested to know that Mr. Engelbert made arrangements for his fortune to be disbursed in two ways. If his heir should choose the money for himself, he would have to wait until his eighteenth birthday. If he should wish to donate the money to a charitable cause, he may do so immediately. And I'm quite sure this school would count as a charitable cause."

Mr. Wallerby turned his attention back to Kam. "So, young man, what do you say? Will you take the money yourself on your eighteenth birthday? Or were you serious when you said you'd use it to save your school?"

Kam looked to his mother. Her hands were clasped beneath her chin. The money would come in very handy when he turned eighteen. It would mean no problem paying for college. It would mean Mom could move out of Gram's house without worrying about finding another job.

Then he looked at his grandmother. The St. Jude alum simply nodded in return.

Kam looked directly at Mr. Wallerby and pointed down to the ground.

Mr. Wallerby raised an eyebrow. "Does that mean you want the money to be used here, at St. Jude's?"

Kam nodded.

Mr. Wallerby turned to Sister Maria Ann. "There's going to be a lot of legal paperwork to be filled out, but

Sister, I think you can safely assume that your school has been saved.

CHAPTER FORTY-ONE

Kam had no idea how long the hugging and cheering and hand clasping went on. People he didn't know shook his hand and congratulated him. Analyn ran right up and gave him a huge hug.

"I'm gonna call Nakia right now," she exclaimed and ran off with her phone.

"Good job, Kam." Vin took his laptop back. "I wish I'd thought of that answer myself. So logical when you think of it."

Sister Maria Ann nearly hugged the life right out of him. "Oh, my dear, dear boy, this school has been my life's work, and I thought it all was going to end tonight. You have no idea what you've done for this old lady."

Mrs. Harris's hug wasn't quite as suffocating. "You should be very proud of yourself, Kameron." She held him at arms' length. "You know, you reminded me of someone tonight. Have you heard of King George VI of England, the father of Queen Elizabeth II?"

Kam shook his head.

"Look him up," Mrs. Harris said, straightening her purple scarf. "I think he'd make an excellent topic for your oral report." She leaned in closer. "He had a little trouble speaking in public, too." She winked at him and walked off to talk with Sister Maria Ann.

The amount of people who wanted to congratulate him was dizzying, but eventually, the crowd began to disperse and Kam's mom insisted on getting him home to bed.

Out in the parking lot, Kam realized he hadn't spoken to one very important person. He'd have to text the message on his phone or use sign language, but somehow he'd get the point across. He whispered in Gram's ear as they reached the car.

"There's someone I need to thank." He wasn't sure if he had said it loud enough for her to hear over the sound of car engines revving to life, but when he pulled away from her face, she smiled at him and nodded.

Back through the school doors, Kam headed for the gymnasium. Old Man Engelbert sat in his motorized chair, chatting with Sister Maria Ann who stood by his side. As Kam approached, Sister looked up. As if sensing the urgency in Kam, she said, "I'll give you two a moment," and stepped aside.

Kam looked at Old Man Engelbert. He was old, wrinkled, and wheezed in each precious breath. How could Kam convey to this man all he'd done for him? Without him, Kam never would've been able to save St. Jude's. He'd be separated from his friends and his favorite teacher.

And then there was the yo-yo. Kam pulled the 1940s Duncan whistler out of his pocket and held it in the palm of his hand. Holding it like that, Kam felt like Old Man Engelbert had given him a piece of his father back.

Kam's mouth opened, and then closed, and then opened again. Each time, he felt the air whoosh out of his body. Never before had he so acutely felt the pain of not being able to talk in school. A simple thank-you on a whiteboard or via text was not enough.

Old Man Engelbert looked up at Kam and smiled. He rested a hand on the arm Kam used to hold out the yo-yo.

"You don't need to say anything, young man," Old Man Engelbert said. "Some things in this world are enough to leave anyone speechless." He closed Kam's hand around the yo-yo.

Kam returned the smile, then threw his arms around Old Man Engelbert. He didn't care who was watching. Some things just had to be done.

Moments later, Kam waved his final good-bye and headed out the door, marveling at the classic Duncan whistler still in his hand.

Steps from the gym door, a hand came down and snatched the yo-yo from him. "Didn't this yo-yo break last week?"

Kam looked up to see T.J. sneering. In his hand, he held the Duncan as if inspecting it in the light. "Oh no, this is a different piece of old junk you've got here." Then he tossed it up and caught it with his other hand.

A volcano erupted in Kam. From deep within him, his fury burst forth. The voice deep within him could not be contained.

"NOOO!"

It was only one word. But it was enough.

The volume, the energy, the sheer force of Kam's word stopped T.J. in his tracks. The sound of the shout reverberated against the gym ceiling far above. It shook the very room and quite possibly the few remaining people in it. Everyone fell silent.

Kam stretched forward and tore the yo-yo from T.J.'s hands. Then he pushed his way through the gym doors and out toward the cool spring night.

Behind him, he was sure, the remaining parents and teachers in the gym were rooted to their spots, watching him leave. As soon as he was far enough away, they would all begin to talk. He could imagine what they'd say.

Was that Kameron Boyd who shouted?

What happened to him not being able to talk? Was that all a joke?

What on earth happened to make him shout like that?

Does this mean he'll talk in school tomorrow?

Kam didn't know the answer to the last question himself. Maybe he would talk tomorrow in school. Maybe he wouldn't.

But one thing was for certain. He'd be at St. Jude's tomorrow—and the day after that, and every school day after that. And he'd be there with Vin, and Analyn, and Nakia, and Mrs. Harris.

And being there with the people he cared about—the true treasures of this world—that was all that mattered.

Note from the Author

But wait! We never answered Vin's riddle. Remember back in chapter 1, when Vin asked Kameron, "Who designed Noah's ark?" Kam never answered the riddle!

Did you figure it out?

If yes, send me the answer at info@ajcattapan.com or find me on Instagram at @a.j.cattapan and tell me what you think the answer is.

Happy riddle solving!

One More Thing

What's that? You think the churches in this book sound pretty cool, and you'd like to visit them? Well, the good news is that all the churches in this book are real (with the exception of Kam's parish, St. Jude's). You can visit all five churches in the Seven Riddles Contest in Chicago and see the artwork in them in person. Just remember to be respectful like the greeter at St. Stanislaus warned Kam and his friends.

Want an organized tour that matches this book? CatholicChurchTours.com has tours that will show you these churches!

About the Author

A.J. Cattapan is a bestselling author, speaker, and teacher living in the Chicago area. Her debut novel *Angelhood* won a Gold Medal in the Moonbeam Children's Book Awards for Young Adult Fiction and an Honorable Mention from Readers' Favorite Book Awards. She's also contributed to several Chicken Soup for the Soul books and had numerous short stories and articles published in magazines for teens and children.

Her goal in writing is to empower young people so that they may live extraordinary lives filled with heart and hope. You can follow her writing adventures at www.ajcattapan.com

Acknowledgements

Thanks to my dad for being my rock through the good times and the bad.

Thanks to my brothers, sisters-in-law, nieces, and nephews for all the love and support you've shown. Your enthusiasm and willingness to help me celebrate each new book are greatly appreciated.

Thanks to my friends who've been my cheerleaders with every book I've released. I'm grateful for all the time you've dedicated to help me throw book launch parties, and all the times you've told random strangers to buy my books.

Thanks to Nell Andrzejewski and the gang at CatholicChurchTours.com. It was during one of her tours that I first learned of some of these churches.

Thanks to the ACFW Scribes who helped to critique this book long before I had the courage to submit it, especially Gretchen E.K. Engel, Marguerite Gray, Linda Samaritoni, Pegg Thomas, Nanci Rubin, Justina Prima, Nancy Kimball, and Stephanie Landsem.

Thanks to my friends at the Catholic Writers Guild who have helped me spread the word, especially Cynthia T. Toney, Theresa Linden, Stephanie Engelman, Stephanie Landsem, Lisa Hendey, Leslea Wahl, and Gina Marinello-Sweeney.

And finally, but most importantly, thanks to my "family" at St. Philip the Apostle School. The doors of the school may be closed now, but you will remain in my heart forever. Long live the Hornets! Even if it's only in our memories.

Dear Reader,

If you enjoyed reading *7 Riddles to Nowhere*, I would appreciate it if you would help others enjoy this book, too. Here are some of the ways you can help spread the word:

Lend it. This book is lending enabled so please share it with a friend.

Recommend it. Help other readers find this book by recommending it to friends, readers' groups, book clubs, and discussion forums.

Share it. Let other readers know you've read the book by positing a note to your social media account and/or your Goodreads account.

Review it. Please tell others why you liked this book by reviewing it on your favorite ebook site like Amazon or Barnes and Noble and/or Goodreads.

Everything you do to help others learn about my book is greatly appreciated!

A.J. Cattapan

Plan Your Next Escape!
What's Your Reading Pleasure?

Whether it's captivating historical romance, intriguing mysteries, young adult romance, illustrated children's books, or uplifting love stories, Vinspire Publishing has the adventure for you!

For a complete listing of books available, visit our website at www.vinspirepublishing.com.

Like us on Facebook at www.facebook.com/Vinspire-Publishing

Follow us on Twitter at www.twitter.com/vinspire2004

and join our announcement group for details of our upcoming releases, giveaways, and more! http://t.co/46UoTbVaWr

We are your travel guide to your next adventure!

The author kindly acknowledges trademark of the following brands:

YouTube—Google Inc. CORPORATION CALIFORNIA 1600 Amphitheatre Parkway Mountain View CALIFORNIA 94043

Google—Google Inc. CORPORATION DELAWARE 1600 Amphitheatre Parkway Mountain View CALIFORNIA 94043

McDonalds—McDonald's Corporation CORPORATION DELAWARE One McDonalds Plaza Oak Brook ILLINOIS 60523

Wikipedia—Wikimedia Foundation, Inc. non-profit corporation FLORIDA 149 New Montgomery Street, 3rd Floor San Francisco CALIFORNIA 94105

Wonder Woman—DC Comics E.C Publications, Inc., a New York corporation, and Warner Communications LLC, a Delaware Limited Liability Company, 2900 West Alameda Avenue Burbank, CALIFORNIA 91505

Made in the USA
Columbia, SC
15 May 2018